The Life of Old Pete

Book Two of *The Drugstore Series*

ALSO BY SD SHELTON

Me, the Crazy Woman, and Breast Cancer

The Drugstore

The Life of Old Pete

Book Two of *The Drugstore Series*

A NOVEL
by

SD Shelton

ENLIGHTEN
PRESS

ENLIGHTEN PRESS
A DIVISION OF ENLIGHTEN COMMUNICATIONS, INC.

Enlighten Press
A Division of Enlighten Communications, Inc.
Norman, Oklahoma

The Life of Old Pete
The Drugstore Series Book Two

First Enlighten Press trade paperback edition November 2017

Manufactured in the United States of America

10 9 8 7 6 5 4 3 2 1

Paperback ISBN 978-0-9825085-5-8
EBook ISBN 978-0-9825085-6-5

Library of Congress Control Number: 2017960697

For more information about special discounts for bulk purchases, please contact Enlighten Press at enlightenpress@cox.net

For my "brothers,"
Robert "Bo" Whitekiller
and Jon "Kip" Whitekiller,
great men who have spent
their lives as Spirit Warriors.

"Humankind has not woven the web of life.
We are but one thread within it.
Whatever we do to the web, we do to ourselves.
All things are bound together. All things connect."

— Chief Seattle

Chapter One

P ete snorted and in doing so, awoke from what had already been a fitful sleep. Even though it was September, it was still blazingly hot, which was normal for Oklahoma. Even though most of the time Pete was cold to the bone, at night in his dreams, he was a robust young man, hunting, fishing and always on the move. His body reacted as if it was so and he would sweat profusely.

Again this morning, after a night in search of a perfect stag, he awoke in puddles of his own perspiration. The warm air that surrounded him didn't help matters.

Most people in the state referred to the first half of the fall season as an "Indian Summer." Being full-blood Cherokee, Pete had heard it all his long life, but only from the white man. He wondered if they had heard about the Cherokee Sun Myth, which told about the Sun's unhappiness with the frowns of the humans in the Middle World, who would look up at her.

"Why don't they know that our drumming made her happy again?" he wondered. It was something that had troubled him for many years, yet he still had not figured it out.

Pete had more than many years to contemplate it. He was older than anyone he knew. He was so old in fact, that he had no idea how old he was. He had stopped counting somewhere back in his late eighties.

Pete lived in an old cabin in a shady grove next to Jumper Creek, near the abandoned train tracks. Jumper Creek was a small, but always running creek, about a half-mile from the little town of Konawa, Oklahoma. Konawa, pronounced Con-Uh-Wah, was located about seventy miles southeast of Oklahoma City, the state's capital. It was right in the middle of Seminole County, where the Seminole Tribe had settled. The town was named by the Seminoles and meant "string of beads." Beads were a form of currency to the tribe and if you had them, you pronounced the word, "Kuh-nah-wah." If you didn't, it was "Con-Uh-Wah." Pete figured the reason the residents settled on the latter was because most folks in the town were not well to do and the pronunciation meaning "without money" fit them much better.

Pete had stumbled upon his old cabin many years before while hunting for new carving stones. Before he found the cabin, he had been living with his sister, Martha. Martha lived across the street from Tinsley's Nursing Home, which was not only a home for the elderly, but also housed the forgotten of society – the mentally handicapped. Because the residents – who most of the town referred to as Tinsleys – were allowed to roam freely, they often interrupted Pete and his sister several times a day.

It seemed the Tinsleys loved company, and especially Old Pete, as he was called by the town residents for as long as he could remember. Many Tinsleys would go up on the rickety old porch while he was there carving wood, stones or fashioning a hunting tool. Most were regulars, but new faces appeared from time to time. Pete couldn't keep track of how many different Tinsleys had climbed their steps. Each would try to engage him in conversation, but he rarely understood what they were trying to say. In that regard, most of the visits were spent with the Tinsleys talking and Pete ignoring them.

Pete had always been a man of very little to no words. His uncles had taught him long ago that listening brought much more power than talking.

"He who keeps his mouth open cannot hear "Unelanvhi's" – the Great Spirit's, whisper," they said.

They also taught him that the Cherokee language had great power so his words should be chosen carefully to help navigate the "vlenidohv," life. Words were to be spoken, and heard, with the upmost respect.

Pete's "edutsi" or uncle and his great-uncle had both been "Didanawisgis," medicine men. Although Pete had not taken that route in life, he could have. He knew almost as much about "nvwoti," medicine, as they did because he had spent most of the first twenty years of his life learning from both men.

Pete learned that everything around him speaks - the grass, trees, animals, water, and stones. His uncles shared that the Great Spirit allowed for the world around him to tell him why things were the way they were. His surroundings could tell him what would change, when it would change, and why. When Pete understood that he could better hear the Great Spirit when his mouth was closed and his ears were open, he began to make it so.

Throughout his life, he also learned that there was much more truth in the language of the world around him than he had ever heard come from men. It was one reason it upset Pete to have the Tinsleys barge onto his porch. They would break the concentration that he used, not only for his chores, but also for his reflective time with the Great Spirit and all the other spirits whom he had known since he was a child.

THE LIFE OF OLD PETE

Carving was a way for Pete to leave the material world, and travel to the place in between where he could meet and converse with the spirits. He learned to travel by carving when he, and the other men of the tribe, sat under the tall pines during the heat of the Oklahoma sun.

As Pete fashioned the endless bounty of wood and stone into beautiful works of art and tools, he found there was something about it that was mesmerizing and calming. It gave his soul peace, and after a time, it led him into deep and introspective trances where he could meet his spirit helpers and "foresee" things to come. It was during one of these trances that he was told part of his purpose in this life was to protect the sick and weak.

However, these spirit helpers were not the only spirits Pete regularly saw. He had been given an extra gift. It was one that he did not tell anyone about for many years; because he was afraid it was actually a curse. Pete could see and talk to the ancestors, who had long left the earthly realm they once inhabited. Moreover, not only could he see his tribe's ancestors, he could also see the spirit of the white man. This, he knew was a curse and he believed that if his fellow tribesmen, or his uncles found out, they would think he had been taken over by a "sgina," an evil spirit.

Somehow, in his heart, Pete knew he was not evil. In fact, his soul was as gentle as feather on the breeze. His heart sang when he was with creation. It burst with love for all he saw. Yet he didn't know how to reconcile the two worlds – the one where he lived and breathed, and the one where things were misty and muted.

It was only when he was nine, and his great-uncle came upon him sitting in his sacred place, that the truth became known.

Pete's favorite place to escape was a flattened boulder hidden inside a curtain of roots that overhung the river near their village. While searching for medicinal plants, the uncle came upon his great-nephew and overheard a conversation. The uncle listened while "Atsilv Awidisgi," Fire Carrier, told Pete why fire was both friend and foe.

"You have been told a great truth," the elder said, walking toward the boy.

Pete was startled, not realizing that his uncle was near.

"You heard this truth?" Pete asked, astonished that his uncle was also able to see Atsilv Awidisgi.

"I did, and now I know you have the gift of sight too," he answered.

"Is it a gift?" the boy questioned.

"It is, as long as you learn who you should see, and who you should not," he looked at the boy, waiting to see if he understood. Pete resumed carving the stone in his hand. He scraped along its hardened edges several moments before finding the courage to confess his secret.

"I see the white man," Pete sighed, bowing his head in shame.

"That is not uyoi. It's not a bad thing," his uncle reassured the boy. "Once our spirit departs this place," the old man gestured to the world around them, "we are given eyes to see."

"I do not understand, Uncle," Pete stopped carving and wrinkled his forehead.

"We cannot see what is real while in this world," his uncle explained, "Only in the next, is truth known."

Pete contemplated the words but still did not comprehend.

"While here, we wear skins that make us think we are separate from one another," his uncle said. "When we die, we shed the skins much like the rattler or a butterfly that emerges from its cocoon. When we shed the layer that separates us, it is then we can see that we are all connected," his uncle took the boy's face into his hands. "We are all one and if we hurt another, we hurt ourselves and we hurt the Great Spirit."

Pete's eyes brightened with understanding.

"So seeing a white man is not bad?" Pete questioned.

"The white man only wore a skin that was white," his uncle continued, "but his spirit is no different from yours. Since he has shed it, he now knows this. He is now able to see how his actions, while in his skin, hurt others. Because he now knows what is udohiyu – true – he will not hurt you."

Pete sat in silence a moment before speaking again.

"I have been able to see many spirits for a long time," he finally admitted. "Sometimes they follow me and I get no peace."

"It is so for me as well," the uncle replied. "It is time for me to teach you the way."

Pete's uncle sat on the boulder beside him and crossed his legs.

"Peter, you can control the communication you have with these spirits." He looked down at the boy. "You have the power to listen when you want to, or to have peace when you need it. I will show you when the new day comes," his uncle promised.

The two sat silently for another moment, Pete weighing his thoughts. "I am glad you know my secret now." He looked up at the gray-haired man.

"I am too," his uncle replied. "It is osdv. It is good."

THE LIFE OF OLD PETE

Pete did in fact learn how to listen when it was needed, and, to tell the many spirits that still roamed the earth realm how to move on. He also learned how to block those that didn't want to leave, but insisted on communicating with him – especially during the night.

Pete came to realize that things were opposite in the place in between. When it was night on Earth, it was light there, and that is why he would be interrupted frequently during the dark hours of the early morning.

Spirits were drawn to those who could see them. When Pete questioned his guides about this, they told him that because of his gift, his soul held a special light. When spirits saw humans with this light, they knew they could communicate with them.

Early on, Pete often wished he did not have the gift. Some of those who had departed insisted on showing Pete how their life had ended. After several reveals, he quickly learned that he did not want to see it. Finally, his spirit guides told him to forbid it. Pete had no idea it was that easy, or he would have done it from the beginning. Apparently there was a rule about communication between this life and the in between. If Pete forbid a reveal or even communication, the souls obeyed his request.

As more spirits came to him, Pete learned things that were unbelievable, but at the same time, made a lot of sense. On many occasions, he found that the spirits just had not known that they were dead. They would wander, confused and looking for loved ones. When he shared with them they were no longer in body, and that the loved ones they sought had already gone to the other side, the soul was finally able to see their own spirit guide. The guide, who had been waiting for the soul to realize he was in spirit form, would then escort them to the Great Beyond.

Pete's sister Martha had often been awakened by Pete talking to the spirits that sought him during the wee hours. She feared that her brother's abilities might cause harm to come to him. Pete reassured her that he was well protected. It wasn't often that Pete would meet with a spirit who was dark, and had blackness or hate in his soul, but if one approached, Pete's "Adanvdo Danuwaanalihi" or Spirit Warrior would step in, protecting Pete from the low energy and banishing the soul from his presence.

Pete met his Spirit Warrior before he had met any other of his spirit helpers. While still just a toddler, he had wandered off on his own. He loved the river near his village, and was determined to explore its rich banks. Pete was almost to the steep and rock encrusted edge when he ran into a very large and noble looking Indian man. The man had appeared out of nowhere, standing with his feet shoulder width apart and his arms crossed in front of his bare chest. He was blocking Pete's way. The Indian wore a beautiful leather and beaded band around his head. Magical glowing feathers fanned out from his crown and light illuminated his entire being.

"Where are you going?" the man asked, without moving his mouth to speak. Pete thought it odd that the man could talk without words. He did not know how to answer, and was a little afraid because he had never seen this man in the village.

As if reading his mind, the glowing being said, "You do not need to fear me. I am Totsuwa, Redbird. I am your Warrior Spirit. I will be with you all your life and will protect you," he told the boy. "You must return to your mother so you will be safe." He pointed toward Pete's home.

Pete did as he was told, never questioning the incident.

It was shortly after that episode that he was introduced to other guides during his sleep, or when he was in a deep trance. Each would visit and tell him who they were and the role they were to play in his life.

Pete met his main guide by leaving his own body and traveling to the other side as he slept. Through the years, he spent as much time in his transcendent world as he did the material one, especially when he needed extra guidance.

During his initial trip, Pete and the guide sat next to an immensely blue lake surrounded by vibrant and astonishing colorful singing flowers. The flowers mesmerized Pete, as they swayed and hummed the richest and most complete tones he had ever heard. Each one glowed with colors that were beyond anything he had ever seen on Earth. It was as if they were lit from within. Although each flower made a different sound, they hummed in perfect harmony, a melody more beautiful than could be imagined.

His main guide had introduced himself as "Unegv Ugidali," White Feather. He told Pete not to tell anyone he could see him or the other spirits, until it was time to be revealed.

"How will I know?" Pete asked the white-haired and cloaked spirit.

"It will be decided for you," White Feather answered. Pete did as he was told and kept the secret until the day his uncle overheard his conversation with Fire Carrier.

Because it had always been a part of his life, and because he actually spent more time conversing with the spirits than he did the living, it caused Pete to be uncomfortable in the earthly world. It was the biggest reason he opted to leave his sister's home – that and an incident with a Tinsley that could have ended very badly.

Many years before, Pete had been listening to his guides explain to him how he could help his sister's husband, Burt. Burt had recently become ill and as Pete was discussing his situation, a Tinsley wandered onto the porch. Pete was so deep into the trance that he neither saw, nor heard, the dwarfish man. The Tinsley got offended because he was being ignored. Feeling insulted, he punched Pete in his chest, startling him badly.

Pete's first instinct was to raise the knife he had been using to carve. Just before he jabbed it into the man, he realized he was in no danger, and quickly lowered it. However, Pete knew then, that he would have to either continue his trances inside the house, which was not an option during the sweltering Oklahoma summers, or he would have to find lodging elsewhere. He remembered the old cabin that sat about a quarter of a mile behind his sister's place and he moved there that night.

Pete never knew who had built or owned the old place, or the land it was on, but in all the years he had been staying there, he never saw another living person. He figured the rightful owners had long since passed on, and there was no one that cared if he made it his permanent home. The cabin consisted of only one room and had no electricity and no plumbing. It did, however, have running water – that of the creek.

The creek was spring fed so the water was always good, except when a couple of years earlier, it had been over taken by salt water that had leaked from an old abandoned oil well site upstream. It caused Pete great hardship because he had to find a way to get water to his place, and that meant carrying it from town in a gallon jug. The worst part was he could only carry one gallon at a time because of his feebleness.

Pete habitually went into town each day. He didn't like to interact with others, but he knew in his heart that he had to go. Not only did the mile walk keep his muscles working, but also, he was now too old to hunt and fish. In addition, Martha had long since crossed to the other side, and this left him no choice but to rely on the stores in town for his sustenance.

After making daily stops at various stores along Main Street, Pete would go behind Ralph's Grocery where there was a water pump. He filled an old distilled water jug that Ralph had given him, before carrying it, and whatever necessities he had picked up that day, all the way back to his cabin. He rationed the water until the following morning when he would do it all over again. Luckily for Pete, because of his age and his weight, which was probably no longer even one hundred pounds, he didn't require much.

At his tallest, Pete had only been five feet five inches. Over the years, with discs compressing, he had become even smaller. In his heyday, however, he easily had thirty to forty more pounds on his small frame, and none of the weight was fat. He had been as lean and muscular as a prizefighter. He was an expert at fishing, hunting and foraging for the fruits and medicinal herbs offered by the land. Also, if he wasn't entranced, he was moving, slinking like a cat through tall underbrush, climbing embankments, and crossing streams.

Pete's mind snapped back to the present. He continued to lie on his bed, noticing a small spider weaving its home in the corner above his head. It reminded him of the ones he watched as a boy growing up in the eastern area of Indian Territory.

Indian Territory was what they called Oklahoma before it had become a state in 1907. His mother and father had been part of the Trail of Tears in 1838, which had relocated numerous Indian tribes to Oklahoma, including over sixteen-thousand Cherokees. Over four-thousand members of his tribe had died in route, including his grandmother on his mother's side, a great-grandfather on his father's side, and his mother's sister who had only been two.

His own mother had been just a baby, and his father, four, when they made the trip. Although very young, his father retained memories of the trip, but did not like to speak of it. When asked, his reply was stark and simple. "Great loss," he would say while bowing his head and shaking it as if trying to release the memories finally.

The members of the tribe, who had made it, mostly settled in the eastern part of the state. They built a community on the western boundary of the Ozark Mountains. They named their settlement Tahlequah, pronounced Tal-lee-qua. Pete had been told that the name came from the Cherokee words tali and yeliquu. Tali, meaning "two," and yeliguu meaning "enough."

Stories of the city's birth name were handed down through the generations of his people. One told of a meeting between the tribe's three chiefs, The Red Chief, The White Chief and the Medicine Chief. The White Chief handled tribal matters in time of peace. The Red Chief acted in time of war, and the Medicine Chief solved any disputes between the other two chiefs.

The meeting was held to decide the location of the Cherokee's permanent capital and took place shortly after settlement. The White Chief did not show up for the meeting. After waiting all day, and with dusk approaching, the Red Chief and Medicine Chief finally declared that two was enough to decide.

A very large group of Cherokee still remained in Tahlequah. Pete found it hard to believe that, some one hundred and thirty-eight years after settling, the tribe had just gotten their first recognized constitution a year earlier in 1975.

"It has taken too many moons," Pete thought to himself.

It was also difficult for Pete to believe that there were so many of his people that chose to stay in a forced land instead of venturing back to the place of their ancestors.

Pete had always wanted to return to Georgia. Throughout his life, he had heard stories of its beauty and the land's riches. However, he had also heard stories of the racism that still existed there. The racism was against not only black people, but also the very people that the white man had stolen the land from – his people, the Great Cherokee Nation.

The one positive about staying in Oklahoma was that the land around their nation's capital was truly beautiful. It was rich with forests, lakes and wildlife. In his mind, he believed that his ancestors' real home must have been similar. It was in believing this, that he was comforted; knowing he would never, at this ancient time in his life, see his homeland.

Chapter Two

Pete lifted his head from the very thin and much worn feather mattress on which he laid. He had fashioned it years ago when he was still a good hunter and had collected feathers from the birds he snared. They included wild turkeys, geese and ducks.

The mattress was comfortable for several years, but age and wear had rendered it barely more than tolerable. He had been lucky that twenty years or so back, he had managed to find an old iron bed frame with springs that someone had dumped into the creek downstream near the old highway. It had taken him most of the day to drag the rusty thing back to his place, but he was glad he had done it. It kept him from sleeping on the ground where snakes, opossums, armadillos and rats sometimes liked to roam.

He had been awakened many times during the wee hours of the morning, with one form or another of the nocturnal pests, foraging through his abode. It also helped shield him from the cold wooden floor during winter, when even the feathers of the mattress and a deer hide could not keep his cold and achy bones warm.

Pete began to rise, which in itself took several minutes. He did not – could not – move as he used to. Every movement he made came with the pain of bones that were long past their prime. He could feel that most of his joints were bone on bone. At his age, he wasn't surprised that whatever it was that used to keep his joints lubricated and moving fluidly, was long gone.

He finally made it to a sitting position, and slowly lowered the sticks, others called legs, over the side of the bed. He looked around to see if anything had been disturbed during the night.

Several weeks earlier, Pete had awoken in the middle of the night to sounds of howling. It was a strange and somewhat unsettling sound. Pete could tell there was a pack of, whatever the creatures were, that were making the noise. However, he could not for the life of him, identify it. He knew it was not coyotes.

Brother Coyote howled in joy, or mourning. He howled in peace, to let others know all was right with the world. No, this howling was harsher and more urgent. The howling that had awoken Pete from a deep sleep was unstable. It was in fact, disturbing. As he listened to its waxing and waning, he worried that it might be lost and long forgotten souls, roaming the darkness in search of a place to call their own. He hoped they would not choose his home in which to reside. It was hard enough to sleep with animals making entry. He did not want to deal with lost spirits too. Pete was glad that he had only heard the howling that one night and it had not interrupted his sleep again. Still, he remained wary that it might resurface.

Pete continued to survey the small and dusty room where he sat. He watched as golden particles filtered through the sunlight that was coming though the east window. They danced across a sunbeam before disappearing into the unlit parts of the room.

Pete then scanned the floor, looking for his current nemesis, a thieving packrat. For the previous two weeks, sister packrat had been thieving anything she could find and hauling it away to what Pete assumed, must be a fully loaded nest.

It seemed the thing that Pete was not able to hide from her – no matter where he put them – were his scissors. The troublesome robber had already stolen three to four pairs of them.

If Pete had a fire going in the old cast iron stove that had remained with the cabin, the animals would stay out. However, because the season had not yet required the stove's warmth, the pests were brazen, and none had been more bothersome than this one.

"What does tsisdetsi do with scissors?" he wondered.

His spirit helpers did not answer, so Pete knew it would remain a mystery to him until they saw fit to enlighten him – if they ever did.

Pete arose slowly and bent to put on the deerskin moccasins he always wore. He didn't understand why most people went to a store to buy their shoes. He could tan a deer hide and get two to three pairs out of one, along with other necessities like a blanket. Each pair he fashioned would last years. Pete didn't think store shoes could do that, even if you paid good money for them.

White people and even some Indians confused him.

"Why do they go to a job day after day to get money for the very things that the Great Spirit provides for free?"

Even when Pete had worked for a living years before, he had never spent money on the things that were already provided to him. He had tried to understand the logic when others did, but again, his spirit helpers had not assisted him. As he looked around at all the things he had been able to make from the hides – a satchel, a seat for his chair, and the blankets, he remained puzzled.

Pete continued dressing in an ancient pair of black Levi's and a khaki, turned grey, button down workman's shirt. In his withered state, both hung from his bony frame and the shirt more resembled a dress. Finally, he donned a long black trench coat.

Martha had bought the coat for him in 1954 at the dry goods store. He had worn the thing sparingly when he first got it, but now it was his most prized possession.

Many years had passed since Pete had lost his ability to retain heat, even during summer. The coat insulated him and if he didn't wear it, he felt as though his entire frozen body would shatter like an icicle falling from the eve of a roof.

In addition, in a sort of spiritual way, the coat made him feel protected. It was as if his sister was still with him when he had to be with the outside world.

Pete combed his long hair, which was more gray than black, and braided it to keep it out of his way. He used to have only one big braid in the back, but the staleness of his bones no longer allowed him to reach behind his head to fashion them. It was all he could do now to divide his hair into two sections and braid it on the sides so he didn't have to lift his arms. The braids hung almost to his waist. Although they used to be longer, a mishap convinced him the he needed to cut them some.

One evening, as Pete leaned over the potbellied stove to throw wood on a dwindling fire, a small log hit the embers. It sent a spark flying into his hair, which caused a braid to catch fire. Before he could put it out, Pete received a minor burn to his face. Since that time, he made sure to keep the braids manageable. It was one reason he needed the scissors. Since they had recently been lifted again, he guessed he would have to get another pair on his trip into town.

Going into town was more than a chore. It made Pete unsettled and almost antsy. He felt as if thousands of eyes were watching him, each wanting to know his secrets.

"Old Pete." That's what they called him and to his face no less. Of course, it was accurate; he was old. He guessed that most people did not mean any real disrespect by it, but it still seemed impolite to him. What if he called Mr. Pendleton, who wore glasses thicker than pop bottles, "Google Eyes" or Lester, the extremely obese policeman, who was as round as he was tall, "Fat Lester?" Wouldn't they take offense? Just because something was true, didn't mean it needed to be spoken aloud.

"It does not matter," his guide, White Feather, reminded him. *"It is not your authentic name."*

Pete agreed, nodding his head. None of the residents of Konawa knew his real name. Only his sister had known it and she was telling no one.

Pete was his grandmother's, on his father's side, first male grandchild. He had come after a long line of granddaughters. Six in fact. After his birth, his grandmother held him and tenderly whispered to him.

"You are Igvyi. You are first," she said, meaning not only that he was her first boy grandchild, but also he was first in her heart. She kissed his head sweetly, "Igvyi, that is your name," she pronounced.

Pete was given his English name by his father. As was Cherokee custom, both the father and the father's mother had naming rights. Knowing firsthand how his people were treated, Pete's father wanted his son to have an English name as well. He hoped that it would help Pete be more accepted by white society. However, not willing to offend his own mother, he gave his son the name Peter.

Missionaries had long ago traveled to the areas in the East where the Cherokees resided. According to his grandparents, they had come to their villages in Georgia and told them of a man named Tsisa who did great things like healing people and bringing them back from the dead. White people called the man Jesus and Pete grew up in his family's Cherokee Church learning about him and his handpicked tribe who were called disciples. Peter was the first one Tsisa named as an apostle.

"You are first to us both," his grandmother told Pete and this had always made him feel special.

Pete slowly shuffled out of the cabin. The sun still had not risen, but its light had come far enough to the horizon to add a glow. Pete figured it was around seven, which would get him to Harvey's Gas Station at his usual time. Pete went to the big Oak tree outside the cabin and relieved himself. It seemed it took much longer these days. His plumbing, he thought, must be as rusty as his bones. When he finished, he began the hour and a half shuffle into town.

Younger folks could have made the walk in fifteen to twenty minutes, but Pete's feet refused to move as they once had. By the time he would arrive in town, he would be hungry and although he would like to go straight to the town's only drugstore to get his morning coffee and breakfast, he couldn't. A stop at Harvey's Gas Station was necessary if he was going to be able to finish the rest of the errands of the day.

Pete liked to get to Harvey's by eight-thirty every morning because it meant that he would have the bathroom to himself. He needed at least fifteen minutes to take care of his business and because the bathroom was a one-holer, he tried to beat the nine a.m. rush so no one would pound on the door and disturb him.

Pete shuffled through the wooded grove he called home and finally made it into the clearing of the pasture behind what used to be Martha's home. An old black dog on the back porch raised his head to look at Pete as he passed, but sensing his gentleness, didn't make a sound.

He had that effect on animals. Their souls could connect with him and they knew he meant no harm. Pete thought to himself that maybe his father and grandmother should have named him Frank, after St. Francis, instead of Peter.

Pete had learned about the Christian saints from his great-aunt, who was Potawatomi and had been educated by Catholic Missionaries. He especially liked St. Francis, not only because of his love of the animals, but also because of his gentle spirit.

"Lord, make me an instrument of Your peace," he recalled the prayer his aunt helped him memorize. *"Where there is hatred, let me sow love; where there is injury, pardon; where*

there is doubt, faith; where there is despair, hope; where there is darkness, light; where there is sadness, joy."

"What more could The Great Spirit want from us?" Pete thought. *"If only we would follow."*

Pete knew the requests of the prayer were entirely possible. He also knew something that it seemed most others didn't. These things could be done just by thinking on them. There was great power in thought and meditation. His helper spirits had taught him this as a child. He learned that manifesting good for his family, fellow tribal members, and his fellow man was not a difficult task – if it was what the Great Spirit wished for too.

Sometimes Pete would think upon things that he wished for himself or others and they would not come to pass. At first, he thought he was doing something wrong, or that the Great Spirit was displeased with him. That is what he thought had happened when, as a young teen, his mother had taken sick and died. Pete had spent days feverishly meditating on his mother's healing. He had not stopped to eat, drink, or go to the bathroom. He carved many pieces of stone and wood into bears, fish, and other various wildlife while in trance, but it had done no good. He felt as if it was his fault that his mother had died. He was heartbroken. But that night, she visited him and explained that no matter how good people were at manifesting on the earth, they could never manifest what the Great Spirit did not intend.

"My mission was complete and He was ready for me to come home," she told Pete. *"It is as it should be."*

Pete learned then that his power would always be limited, and that was how it was meant to be.

Thinking about St. Francis and his mother, had again put him into a trance and he "awoke," just a short distance from Harvey's. He was now inside the town and there were sidewalks on which to travel. Pete would almost blow over sometimes as the few cars that traveled the old highway where he walked, came whizzing by. After, he would regain his footing and proceed toward his destination, his worn moccasins making a soft scratching sound with each step.

He crossed the gravel parking lot, passed the gas pumps and headed toward the men's room, which was located on the east side of the small building. The two bays for repairing automobiles were closed but he could see one of old man Harvey's grown sons inside the store area, straightening things around the cash register. He lowered his head so that, if the man saw him, he would not have to acknowledge him.

Pete stepped up onto the concrete sidewalk, which led into the men's room and slowly pushed open the door. It was heavy and he feared it wouldn't be long before it would be too much for him to handle.

Pete knew he wasn't a minute too soon in getting there. He felt as if he was about to come unhinged from his discomfort. He closed the door and fumbled with the latch trying to secure it. Then he headed straight toward the sink, stopping just short of the counter, and adjacent to the air hand dryer, which hung on the wall. He pushed the button and slowly began rubbing his frozen hands underneath the warm air that escaped.

Pete stood there thawing his bony, brittle hands until the almost unbearable ache began to subside. When the dryer stopped, he pushed it again and continued the thawing process. It usually took about fifteen times to stop the shooting, throbbing pain that infiltrated the skeletal appendages. Pete was very grateful for the dryer, which had only been installed a few years earlier. Before that, he would stand and run his hands under warm water from the faucet.

When the dryer shut off and Pete's hands were sufficiently warmed, he unlocked the door, struggled to get it open and then shuffled outside on his way to the drugstore.

Chapter Three

Lester, the town's only policeman, was sitting in the gravel parking lot in his police cruiser as Pete shuffled by the passenger side.

Lester liked to sit at the end of Main Street, and watch the comings and goings in town. However most of the time, Pete noticed, he was really just sleeping. This morning though, Lester was drinking coffee and staring off down the street, as if he were deep in thought. If he even saw Pete, he didn't acknowledge it. Pete figured that Lester was thinking about the recent rash of robberies that had been happening to some of the town's elderly residents.

One day while in Pendleton's Grocery, Pete had overheard a patron telling Bubba Turner, the butcher, that Lester had to call in help from Oklahoma City because he had not been able to solve the crime spree. Pete was not surprised that Lester needed help.

Pete himself had been arrested by Lester from time to time and had never been sure why. However, not wanting to bring attention to himself, he just went along peacefully and served whatever time Lester thought was appropriate, which was never more than a day.

Pete actually didn't mind serving time because he was fed pretty well and had a good bed with a semi-comfortable mattress upon which to sleep. Also, if he stayed overnight, it meant that he didn't have to make the long trek into the town the next morning because he was already there.

It seemed that Lester got frustrated with Pete though, because after Pete was arrested, he wouldn't answer questions. Pete wasn't trying to be difficult; he just didn't really understand what Lester was trying to coax from him, and because he didn't know, he couldn't answer. The whole interrogation was pointless and Pete did not want to waste his words. They were too precious.

Pete crossed the street, which ran perpendicular to Main Street. It was actually the real Main Street, but everyone called Broadway, Main. Pete had no idea why this was so. Maybe it was because it was where most of the town's stores and the post office were located.

After inching his way across the road and onto the sidewalk in front of Glenn's Lumber, he began his journey toward his next stop, halfway up the second block. As he walked, Pete thought about how his history had begun with Lester. As a younger man, he had never been in trouble with the law. Only in his old age did he have run-ins. They had always been with Lester. In fact, it had only been since a few years ago when he started coming into town every day.

After his sister died, Pete managed to keep taking care of himself by way of the land, but one day he awoke, dressed and strolled out into the early light of dawn, hoping to snare a rabbit.

Brother Rabbit liked to graze early and Pete knew exactly where. Further north of Pete's cabin was a small pond with a grassy knoll where the rabbit and his family had a nice den under the sage that grew there. Pete hunted by the code that he never took more than he needed. He wouldn't take an entire family, even if he knew he could.

Pete was an expert at finding rabbit burrows. With the animals being prolific reproducers, that could have as many as six litters a year, he didn't need to return to the same nest more than twice during a season. Pete did not take a life without giving thanks to the animal's soul for its great sacrifice. He also thanked the Great Spirit for providing it.

Pete was always careful not to get the mother. Mothers grazed close to the nest while bucks branched further out.

While he had several ways of hunting, including traps, he found that many times, other animals, especially the coyotes, could get to an animal before he could, so he relied mostly on a small twenty-two caliber rifle, or his bow.

On this morning though, Pete came upon the knoll after slinking through some tall underbrush, only to find that the moment he spotted his buck, it spotted him and sprinted off into the brush on the opposite side of the pond. It darted before Pete could even begin to reach for his rifle.

"That is odd," Pete thought to himself. *"How did he see me?"* Pete had never had it happen. He was always so quiet that even the wind mistook him for its own echo.

Pete visited several more rabbit nests until the sun was too high and the rabbits had burrowed. At each one though, the same thing occurred, and he had to go home empty handed.

The following morning, Pete tried to snare a guinea in a thicket. However, the bird sensed him coming while he was still about twenty yards away. It squawked, alerting all the others, who immediately dispersed.

Again Pete went home empty handed and by day three when a second try at a rabbit proved as futile as the first, Pete realized that the hunting power he had been given for all of his life, had run its course. When thinking about it, Pete decided he shouldn't have been surprised. He had already outlived everyone in his family, so it was not odd that he would outlive his abilities. When he questioned his guides, they affirmed what he believed.

"It is so," they said.

Hungry, Pete meditated on what to do. *"Go to town,"* the helpers told him. He did and had been doing so ever since. Back then, Pete hoped that his journey on this side would end soon so he would not have to continue to make the trip. It didn't. He had been going into town for years and he showed no signs of leaving the earth soon.

Pete remembered the first time Lester arrested him. He had been coming into town a little over a month. He was at Ralph's when Lester came in, walked up to him and asked him what it was he thought he was doing. Pete looked at Lester as if he didn't understand – which he didn't.

"I'll ask you again," Lester said, pointing to an apple in Pete's hand. "What do you think you are doing?"

Pete thought it was obvious. He was getting an apple. *"Why is it hard to see?"* Pete thought to himself. *"Surely, he does not want me to tell him I am getting an apple because it will make him look very dim and I do not want to embarrass him,"* Pete thought. Therefore, Pete did not answer.

"So that is how you are going to play this?" Lester asked.

Again, Pete did not know how to answer him.

"What does he mean by play?" Pete questioned himself. *"Is he asking me if I can play this apple like an instrument? Surely, he does not think I can play an apple,"* Pete thought. *"I wonder if he is alright."*

Pete took another moment to run the question through his mind again, but it still didn't make sense to him. Meanwhile Lester took Pete's empty hand and slowly turned him around.

"Give me the apple," Lester told him, which Pete did. "If you aren't going to tell me what you are doing with the apple, then you have to come with me," Lester said as he put some sticky handcuffs on Pete's wrists.

"Lester must have had pancakes this morning," Pete thought to himself as the smell of syrup wafted up to his nose from the cuffs.

Lester escorted Pete as he slowly shuffled up the produce aisle, and past the two registers in the store. Lester stumbled along behind him, trying not to run him over.

"Tell Ralph I'll take care of it," He told Betsy, one of the store's cashiers.

"I will," Betsy said, scoffing at Pete as he went past.

Lester walked Pete across the street to the police station. Pete noticed that many people were standing outside the stores looking at them. Pete began to look around too to see what they were watching. He didn't see anything out of the ordinary, so he lowered his head and continued walking, watching his feet to make sure he didn't trip.

When Lester took him into the one room Police Station that was located inside City Hall, he sat him in a small metal folding chair that faced the station's counter.

"You just sit there while I get this paperwork done," he told Pete, as he helped him slide onto its cold surface.

Pete watched as Lester went behind the counter and began pecking on an old typewriter. Lester hunted and pecked for about ten minutes while Pete, bored with the whole process, began to nod off.

The loud ringing of the telephone startled Pete awake. He didn't know how long he had been asleep.

"Oh." Lester said into the receiver. "Oh, okay," he eyed Pete as he spoke. "Well that's okay then, isn't it?" He asked whoever was on the other end. "Okay. I'll take care of it. I 'preciate the call."

Lester hung up the phone. "Dad gummit," he said, pulling the paper out of the typewriter, wadding it up and throwing it away.

"Come on Old Pete," Lester said while helping him to his feet. "Let me help you back across the street."

Pete slowly arose and Lester took the handcuffs off him. He held Pete steady as he directed him out the door and back toward Ralph's. Lester helped Pete up a large step, which ran along the curb in front of Ralph's and then let him go.

"You stay out of trouble Old Pete," he said. Pete kept his head fixed on his feet and nodded, then shuffled back into the grocery store.

"Lester must be having some mental problems," Pete thought to himself as he started back down the produce aisle.

Chapter Four

Pete crossed the side street between the auto store and the two stall carwash. Then he stopped to look at the poster on the wall of the little one screen movie theater. *Dog Day Afternoon* was playing. Pete wondered what the movie was about. There was a picture of a man with a gun in front of some old-timey stores. Pete thought the town in the picture looked like it could be Konawa or even Maiden, a city about 15 miles to the south. The poster said that the man was robbing a bank and the people would never forget what took place.

Pete remembered when Pretty Boy Floyd had robbed the First National Bank of Konawa. He didn't remember the exact year but he knew it was in the early 1930's, because it happened within the first few of years of him moving to Konawa with Martha and Burt.

"I was an old man then," Pete thought to himself. *"Who knew I would still be here now?"* he sighed while silently praying for the Great Spirit to release him from his earthly duties.

Burt had helped put up electric lines for Oklahoma Gas and Electric beginning in 1917 when the electric company expanded its service to eastern Oklahoma. Bill got Pete a job with the company shortly after, and together, along with Martha, they moved around with the company putting up lines. They ended up in the area of Konawa in the late 1920's when Burt, who was already in his mid-fifties, became ill.

Burt knew he had to stop working. He wanted to make sure Martha would have a place when he passed, so they took the money they had saved, along with some savings that Pete had accumulated, and bought a tiny house in Konawa. The house was in a good location for Pete because of the close proximity to Jumper Creek where he could get stones and because of the fields around it where he could get an abundance of medicinal herbs and plants.

Pete had been able to keep Burt alive for many more years using the herbs, plants and the medications he and his spirit helpers created. Nevertheless, the time finally came when White Feather told Pete that the Great Spirit was ready to bring his brother-in-law to the other side. Pete reluctantly told Martha and her husband the news. Burt asked Pete to promise to look out for Martha and he agreed. Even after Pete had moved out of the house, he made sure to check in on her every day, and when she herself had become ill years later, he moved in with her again. He cared for Martha the same way he had his brother-in-law until White Feather told him it was time to help her cross.

As she lay in her bed on the last day of her stay on Earth, Martha told Pete that Tsisa was there at her feet, along with Burt, their mother, father, aunt and their other sisters who had already crossed over. It was strange to Pete that she could see them but he could not. He was always the one who saw those from the other side. Yet he had never seen his own loved ones, with the exception of his mother the one time. It made Pete a little jealous, but he was glad that she was not going to be alone on her journey.

When she passed, Pete, with the help of the women at her church, took her body and dressed it in her beautiful ceremonial stomp dance skirt and blouse. Then, they wrapped her in a deerskin, and he and some of the churchmen buried her next to her husband on the grassy knoll near the pond by Brother Rabbit's burrow.

Pete looked at the movie poster again. He wondered how the story would end, but he knew he would never find out. Pete had gone to the movie in Maiden about fifteen years earlier with Martha and her friend from the High Springs Seminole Indian Church. The church, which his sister attended regularly, was a couple of miles north of Martha's house. When Martha had to stop driving because of poor eyesight, her friend Hannah picked her up and brought her home each week.

Pete, Martha and Burt had been only a handful of Cherokees in the area, so there was no Cherokee church for them to attend. However, the Seminoles had welcomed them into the church community and after finding out about Pete's gifts, many of the members went to Pete for health issues.

One Sunday after church, Martha told Pete that Hannah had invited them to go see a movie about the great Apache warrior Geronimo. Pete had studied Geronimo when he attended the Cherokee Male Seminary, a tribal college and one of the first institutes of higher learning established west of the Mississippi.

Geronimo's real name was Goyathlay or "One who yawns." Pete greatly admired the Apache's courage, intellect and convictions, so he told Martha he would like to go.

Within the first moments of the movie, the Captain of the U.S. Military told his lieutenant that the Apaches were nothing but a pack of wild and dirty animals. Pete, embarrassed, looked around the theater. He was glad that it was a Tuesday evening and the audience was small. Although he saw no one looking at Martha, Hannah or him, he felt like all eyes were on them, judging them as dirty animals. Pete did not want to see any more of the movie, but his sister continued to watch, so Pete did also.

When the Indians met the soldiers, Pete noticed that they did not look like real Indians. Not only didn't they look right, but they didn't talk right either. In fact, they didn't resemble Indians in any way. Instead, they walked, talked and acted like white people. When the first close up of Geronimo came, Pete's suspicions were confirmed. The person playing Geronimo had blue eyes.

In all his years, Pete had never seen any Indian with blue eyes. Some Indians, who were not full blood, could have green eyes or dark gold, but not blue.

It wasn't long before Pete realized he had seen this actor before on television. After Martha had purchased a small television from Hibbs' Appliance Store, she and Pete would sometimes watch *The Rifleman*. Geronimo was actually Lucas McCain.

This movie reminded him of the television show. After seeing a couple of episodes where the Indians were portrayed as criminals, or worse, Pete became upset and told Martha he didn't want to see it any more. She agreed.

Like the movie, the television show didn't portray the tribes accurately. Most, if not all the Indians Pete had known during his life were very good people. They were kind. They cared about one another and they respected the world around them. He didn't think it was fair to still be shown as "savages" when they were anything but. In fact, Pete felt as though the TV show and movie makers were hypocrites. Pete could give a thousand examples of how the early white settlers had been much more savage than any of the Indians.

As he continued watching the movie, Pete became more uncomfortable. In the first ten minutes alone, Indians had been called animals and even devils several times. Pete did enjoy the part where Geronimo told the storekeeper that he was not an animal that needed to be branded. Nevertheless, as it was in history, the man used a gun to force Geronimo to be subservient. It was not right.

The movie also made the Indians look ignorant and stupid and showed the Apaches laughing at the idea of reading books. Pete knew there was no truth to this. The wisest people he had ever known were the Cherokee elders. They had taught him what it meant to be a steward of the earth and a steward to others. The elders in the Seminole church they attended did the same. Moreover, Pete and all of his family could read, even his mother and father. Not only could they read and write English, but they also could read and write Cherokee, and Pete himself had graduated Cherokee Male Seminary before it had closed in 1898. In addition to English, he had studied Latin and French. Most of the white people he knew could only speak one language – could only read or write one language. Along with the languages, Pete and his fellow students studied algebra, astronomy, geography, philosophy and even zoology. That alone should have proven the intellect of the tribes. He did not – could not – understand why Indians were being shown in this light.

Pete hoped that not all people believed this was true, because it wasn't even close. In fact, it was so far removed from all reality, Pete was in utter disbelief. The longer the movie continued, the crazier it got – especially when it implied the U.S. Calvary, and the missionaries, had taught the Indians how to grow corn. It was from the white man's own history books that Pete had learned the first white settlers would have starved to death if the Indians had not taught them how to grow corn and beans.

It was true that the movie did show how promises made to the Apaches were broken and how their land was taken. However, it seemed implied – because of the continual way the group was characterized – that they deserved it.

Pete also noted that the movie neglected to show the government broke, not only its first promise to the Apaches regarding land, but also many other promises. One of the biggest being Geronimo's final surrender in 1886.

Instead of allowing the tribe the land promised, the government sent them to confinement at military forts in Florida and later Alabama. It was there that many of the tribal members died from tuberculosis and other illnesses. Pete didn't agree with all the killing in which that Geronimo took part. He felt it was better to solve problems through peace, although he hadn't figured out how they could have accomplished that. He did however, understand the anger the warrior must have felt after finding his family massacred.

Pete, himself, had never married, and he didn't have children, but he knew what love was. He loved his own family to every depth of his being. He wondered if losing them at the hands of others would have caused an anger and hate so intense that he could murder. He hoped not, but he could not be sure.

The longer the movie progressed, and the falsehoods continued, the more anxious about leaving Pete became. He continued watching Martha, hoping that she or Hannah would make a move to go, but they remained seated, as stoic as statues.

Pete's heart hurt, knowing that no one with them in the theater was being told the truth.

"It is not right to justify hate," he thought.

When Pete and the two women got into the car and began discussing the picture, Martha told him how horrified she was at what she had seen. Pete told her he felt the same and asked why she didn't leave.

"I was afraid." she bowed her head in sorrow. "I thought if we got up and people saw us, they might say something bad because of what was shown."

Pete understood her reasoning. The thought had crossed his mind too. After seeing that film, Pete never made the mistake of going to a movie again.

"I do not want to nourish even make believe hate. There is already enough of it that is real."

Chapter Five

Pete continued his journey, passing Fran's Grocery and Tag Agency. He had only gone into the small store one time, shortly after he started going into town. On that day, Pete opened the cloudy glass door and entered. He stood at the front and looked all around to see if there was something there he should get for himself or his place.

"Well hello!" Fran, or at least who he assumed must be Fran, had said to him as she stood up from behind a dusty old desk. Fran wore a big smile on her face and acted as if Pete had been a long lost friend coming home.

This confused Pete because he didn't think he had ever met the woman, who looked to be in her late seventies. She had on a pretty blue cotton dress, and her gray hair was pulled up in a bun. Pete looked at her more closely while fishing through his memory to find something he recognized. The woman wore cat eyeglasses, which Pete thought, actually made her look somewhat cat like. Still, he couldn't produce a memory that contained her.

"Is there something I can help you with?" she swung her arm around the store like a game show hostesses showing off a prize.

Pete did not answer her and instead looked down at his moccasins. Fran must have sensed he was uncomfortable so she took the lead.

"Well you just feel free to look around then," she said, sitting back down. "I'm working on a tag request here," she said pointing to her old typewriter. "You just let me know if you need my help."

Fran buried her head in her paperwork, and much like Lester, hunted and pecked her way through the sheet of paper in her machine.

Pete already knew there was nothing there he wanted or needed because, well – there was nothing there. He thought from the sign out front that this was a grocery store, but all Pete saw were a couple of old apples and a banana well past its prime. They sat in a refrigerated produce case that didn't work.

Other than the pieces of fruit, there were no other groceries, only some very dusty trinkets on a shelf toward the back of the store. Pete was sure he wouldn't have any use for those items, however with the woman's warm greeting and the obvious pride she had for her store, Pete felt obligated to look around, so as not to hurt her feelings.

Pete shuffled toward the shelves in the back to get a closer look at the things stashed there. He looked over his shoulder back at Fran, watching her as she continued pecking at the typewriter. It was then he realized who she was. Although he didn't know her, he had seen her before when she was a passenger in a purple car that had almost run him over on several occasions.

Part of Pete's journey into town each day, had to be walked on the side of the small two lane road which led into town. It didn't seem dangerous to him, as most people drove slowly and the drivers seemed to watch out for him because they would veer wide as they passed. On the third day of his new routine though, an old silver-haired woman in the purple car did just the opposite.

Pete had been walking for only a short while when he heard a car coming from behind. He didn't pay it any mind until he heard gravel. Pete knew the only place there was gravel was on the side of the road and the only thing on the side of the road, was him. He turned to see the purple car, about one hundred yards away, barreling toward him. He stepped off onto the grass in front of Tinsley's trying to get out of the car's way. At first, the car looked as if there was no driver. When it got closer though, Pete could see a big tuft of silver hair sticking out over the steering wheel and little silver glasses peering through it.

The car continued its trajectory toward him, and Pete backed away from the road until he found himself against the chain link fence that surrounded the nursing home.

"This must be it," Pete thought to himself. "The Great Spirit is finally going to let me come home."

Pete was wrong though. At the last second, small-withered arms jerked the steering wheel to the left and the purple car left the grass, crossed the gravel and righted itself unto the concrete road. Pete watched as the car continued down the highway, left of center until it rounded the curve into town and he could see it no more.

Pete's heart had never raced as quickly as it had then. It was beating even faster than it had when he was a child on an exciting hunt with his father. He took in a deep gulp of air and then exhaled.

"Well, maybe next time," he thought as he shuffled back toward the roadside to continue his journey. Upon further reflection though, Pete decided he didn't want to travel to the other side via a purple car. He would much rather go peacefully in his sleep.

He surmised that in order to avoid death at the hands of the silver poof-haired woman, he would have to become vigilant when he heard the sound of gravel behind him. Unfortunately, it turned out to be often.

Only a few days later, the woman passed him traveling the opposite direction as Pete. Moments later, he heard her returning as the familiar sound of tires on gravel enveloped his ears. He learned, after many encounters like that one, that when she came back, she would have with her at least two children. One day though, he had seen her with Fran.

That day, Pete had heard the familiar gravel sound and turned to see the tiny driver barreling toward him. Fran grabbed the steering wheel and redirected it back onto the road, causing the car to leave the gravel long before it normally would have. Pete wondered if the woman thought she had saved him and maybe it was why she seemed so happy to see him.

Pete continued surveying the odds and ends on the shelf. It wasn't long before something caught his eye. It was a stick about eight inches long with a bulbous end and something painted on it. He picked it up and it rattled. It wasn't like a baby's rattle or even a ceremonial rattle like the tribal members used when they danced. Those were made from a turtle's shell. This one was wooden. Pete shook the thing and it rattled more. Then he dusted if off, revealing the painting more clearly. There was a girl with long black hair, similar to all of his sisters' hair. The painted woman wore a necklace made of flowers and a very revealing top that appeared to be nothing more than a brassiere. She also wore a grass like skirt that showed her navel. Pete was a little embarrassed by the scantily clad woman, but her beauty reminded him of his own beautiful mother.

Pete thought he remembered seeing a little statue of this woman or one like her on the dashboard of Festus Marney's pickup truck. He wondered if she was famous.

Pete fingered the rattle and shook it again. It made a nice sound, like a hard rain falling. He had never had a rattle because he was not a ceremonial dancer as Martha had been. He looked back again at the store's owner, wanting to ask her how much it cost. He debated on interrupting her work but it appeared that whatever she was doing was very important.

Pete shook the rattle once more and closed his eyes listening to its song. It really did sound like rain. If he shook it slowly, he could make it sound like a soft rain and, with harder movements, could change it to a soaking rain. Pete actually began to go into a trance from listening to it.

"Do you like that?"

Fran jolted him from the trance.

Pete turned to her and nodded that he did.

"Well you can have it. That thing has to have been here at least 30 years," she said.

Pete did not want her to give it to him so he began to take his little leather money pouch from the pocket of the trench coat. As he pulled it out, the woman stopped him.

"Oh no." She waved his hand away. "I couldn't charge you for that old thing. Why I should pay you for getting it out of here. I think one of my boys brought that back from Hawaii after serving there. I thought it was awfully cute when he first brought it, but really, how many times can you rattle the thing before it just becomes a nuisance?" she asked.

Pete thought that he could rattle it forever and it would never be a nuisance. To him it was a magical and beautiful thing. Not only did it remind him of his mother, but it also made rain. There were few things that could be more wonderful than that.

Pete shyly smiled at her and put his pouch away. He put the maraca into his other deep pocket before slowly shuffling out the door.

"You come back again now," he heard Fran say as he left. He didn't think he would - and he hadn't - but he remained grateful to her.

Chapter Six

Pete continued his slow but steady trip up the street. He passed the Cut and Curl, which was usually full of blue-haired ladies, some in large pink rollers. This day however, it was too early because the shop had not yet opened.

When he would pass the place, usually on his way back home, he tried not to look into the window. If he did, all the ladies would wave and make a fuss. Pete didn't understand it. He didn't know any of them except by reputation.

From time to time, Martha would point a woman out and tell Pete something about her. Martha never said anything bad about any of them. In fact, she told Pete things like, "That's Mrs. Roberts. She makes a delicious Bundt Cake," or "Oh look, there's Mrs. Flanders. She's just the sweetest thing." Pete really couldn't even remember who was who.

Now that Martha was gone, Pete didn't hear much about anyone. Sometimes, he would hear things when he was going in and out of the town's stores, but he tried to pay no attention. He knew that most everything folks believed about others was only superficial at best, and completely false at worse. It was a downfall to living in such a small community. People had nothing better to do, so they made their entertainment by talking about their neighbors.

Pete had even heard things about himself that were just plain crazy. One afternoon, after Lester had arrested him yet again for something unknown to him, a twenty-year-old delinquent named Danny Browder was brought in. As soon as Lester put him into the second and only remaining cell, which was directly across the hall and facing Pete, Danny sauntered to the door to see who was in Pete's cell.

The kid pointed to Pete.

"Hey, you're that Voodoo guy," the dingy looking guy said, taking a few steps backwards as if he were afraid.

Pete looked at him, cocking his head to see if he had heard him correctly.

"I don't want no trouble," Danny said, holding his hands out in front of him, as if trying to ward off an oncoming train.

Pete still did not understand. Did he think that Pete was a Raven Mocker, the most dreaded of all Cherokee Witches?

The Raven Mocker appeared in the night to take the life of the sick and add it to its own life so that it could remain alive. Pete knew Raven Mockers looked old and withered because of all the lives they had added to their own. It was true that Pete looked old and withered, but he had never taken a life, especially in order to keep his. He didn't want any more life as the current one had already been too long. Pete became visibly upset that this person – maybe even the town – thought he was a Raven Mocker.

Danny saw the distress in Pete's old face.

"You know if you want to do that Voodoo stuff, that's your business," he tried to placate Pete in hopes that the old man wouldn't put a curse on him. "I ain't got no complaint with it. It's your business," he repeated.

Pete shook his head no, trying to get the skinny and disheveled fellow to understand that he wasn't a Raven Mocker or a Voodoo guy.

"Like I said, it ain't no un's business but yours." Danny backed up to the far end of his cell, putting as much distance between them as he could.

"I'm not," Pete solemnly stated. "I don't take lives."

"I don't know 'bout killin' no one…" Danny said, not understanding the Raven Mocker idea Pete had gotten into his head, "…but you sure you aren't the Voodoo guy? You sure look like the Voodoo guy." Danny raised a questioning eyebrow. "Isn't that your trench coat?" he pointed to the black coat that Pete was still wearing.

Pete looked at his coat and nodded that it was. "I don't practice Voodoo," he repeated.

"Is it witchcraft then?" the young man asked.

Pete had already told him he wasn't a witch. Why did he keep asking? He again shook his head no.

"Well what is it then?" Danny's curiosity made him forget his uneasiness and he went to the bars facing Pete.

"I am Christian," Pete told him.

"Well I'll be!" Danny snorted and slapped a bar on the cell. "You don't fool around with that hoo doo Voodoo? Well I'll be! I been told all my life to be careful if I saw you 'cause you could do curses and shit on people. I always been afraid of you. I guess my friends was just funnin' me," he chuckled.

Pete starred at him blankly.

"Is that what people say about me?" he asked himself. He became horrified at the idea until White Feather intervened.

"It is not," Pete was told. *"And even if it was, what concern is it of yours?"*

Pete knew White Feather was right. What others thought of him was none of his business. He knew there was but one judge and Pete had tried to live in the material realm the same way he would have lived if face to face with the Great Spirit.

There was no doubt he had fallen short throughout his life. He could become angry, especially when he was younger and other people would stare at him and his family.

He remembered occasions when they had gone into town to buy supplies, and a white mother steered her children away from them. Other times, people acted as if they had a wretched, contagious disease and would back up against a building to let Pete's family pass. Pete could see the pain and shame in the eyes of the women he fiercely loved, and it caused a powerful rage to well up inside him. His only solace was that he hadn't been angry for himself. He was angry that the best women he had ever known, were being treated disgracefully. It was heartbreaking.

Pete wanted to shake those people and ask them why they had to make his mother and sisters feel bad. White Feather and his other spirit helpers would come to him and teach him the way of forgiveness and understanding.

"They don't know who you really are. They don't know who they really are." White Feather told Pete, reiterating his great-uncle's explanation about people's skin causing them to believe they were separate.

Pete would acknowledge his anger and then release it, thus taking the power from it. He wished that he had been able to keep at bay all the time, but inevitably, he would fail and have to repeat the process.

Pete sighed remembering Danny Browder and the others, as he continued on his way. He passed what used to be the old mercantile building, which now stood mostly empty except for some wooden crates and a large, rusted counter scale.

The mercantile had been one of the most popular stores on the street from the turn of the century through the 1950's. When the grocery stores began selling pre-packaged beans, flour, rice and coffee, business slowed down. The store was able to stay open because a few people still liked buying in bulk and didn't completely trust "new and improved." However, after the big tornado, the owners, decided to retire.

The mercantile wasn't the only store affected by the tornado. Several of the town's other businesses decided either not to rebuild or to move to Maiden where there was more people to buy their wares. It was the beginning of the population decline of the town.

There were so many years under Pete's belt that he had long since given up trying to remember specific dates. He couldn't remember exactly when the tornado had hit, although he knew it was early in the 1960's. He also remembered that it had not occurred during the spring or early summer, which was known as tornado season. Instead, it had come sometime during the winter. What he did remember was that it was big, and he knew it was coming because his spirit helpers told him so.

Unlike most, Pete understood that tornados and other natural disasters were not necessarily harmful or bad but many times served a purpose. Pete asked his guides if he could speak to the storm before it came. They agreed.

"What are your intentions?" Pete asked the storm.

"There are things that need to be cleansed," it answered. *"There are those who need to take stock of what is important and those who need to come together."*

Not all the storm's answers were Pete's to know, but it was revealed that it would be big and most likely, devastating.

"I ask that you have mercy on this land and its people," Pete humbly pleaded. *"I do not wish to interfere with your mission, but if it can be accomplished without loss of life, I will be grateful."*

"Because you are respectful of my ways and because you have served the Great Spirit for your lifetime, it is agreed," the storm answered. *"I will delay my arrival."*

THE LIFE OF OLD PETE

Pete was unsure of what that meant until after the storm hit. At 6:55 p.m., it trekked through the southwest quadrant of the city, near the school. It hit the First Baptist Church and several other buildings in the last block of Main Street and many houses south of it. It ripped a wide path through the community and damaged or destroyed two-thirds of the homes and businesses. The aftermath looked like a war zone.

Upon seeing it, Pete understood the agreement. Had the storm hit earlier, the town would have been full of people and the loss of life would have been great. It even leveled one of the cafés, but left the patrons, who hunkered under a counter, completely unscathed. Overall, only five people in the entire town were slightly injured with cuts and scrapes.

Pete asked his guides to pass along to the storm his gratefulness.

The storm's mission was revealed in the aftermath too. It cleansed the town of some of the more dilapidated buildings and almost every resident came to someone's aid. Some searched, some provided supplies, others gave food and shelter and hundreds helped clean up the debris. The townsfolk united in what can only be described as the perfect example of loving your neighbor as yourself. More than that, it gave a grateful heart to the residents of the community, who all took stock of their lives.

They were shown the things that were important and should be cherished. Mothers held their children tighter. Husbands looked more adoringly at their wives. Brothers and sisters stopped fighting and neighbors stopped bickering. The town became aware that its people were not separate entities operating independent of one another, but instead, each of them was needed to make the community what it was. The loss of even one would have changed them forever.

Although the event was traumatic, many would later say that it could be considered a blessing. The town's residents were closer than they had ever been.

Chapter Seven

Pete was nearing his second stop and his hands were beginning to seize up again from the cold. He wished he were able to make his rounds more quickly because the cup of coffee from the drugstore had a multipurpose use. The steaming cup would not only warm his insides, but also his hands, making it possible for him to complete the rest of his errands.

Pete walked past another vacant storefront. He thought he remembered that at one time it had been a bar similar to the Red Door, which he had passed in the previous block. It was named the Blue Door and both bars had their glass doors painted to match their respective color. Pete wondered why the Red Door had survived and the Blue Door had not. He also wondered if it had anything to do with patrons preferring one color to the other. He himself was partial to blue.

Many times, when Pete passed the remaining bar in the morning, the owner was just locking up from the night before. He would assist the last couple of customers out the door, telling them he would see them again that night.

Pete didn't really know any of the patrons except Bengal Billy, whom he had seen in the jail one time when Pete had also been there. Billy was also a full blood Indian, but he was a Seminole. Pete had seen him at the church whenever he had attended with Martha, and he always looked to be sober. People said that Billy had once been a Golden Gloves Boxing Champion, but the drink and possibly some left over memories of the Vietnam War had taken their toll.

Pete did not like the drink, although as a young man he had tried it. White Lightning they called it. It had come from a distillery deep in the forests around Tahlequah and his uncles brought it to him and told him to drink. Pete couldn't have been more than sixteen at the time.

"Take this," his uncle said, handing him an old brown bottle. "Drink it."

Pete knew better than to question his elder, so he did as he was told. Pete felt as though he had set himself on fire with the first swallow. It spewed from his mouth and nostrils and he coughed and choked until he thought he would pass out. Every time he tried to calm himself and get a breath, the fire would ignite again when the air reached the back of his throat. Pete hit his knees and then fell to all fours before his uncles helped him up and ordered him to drink again.

Pete wanted nothing to do with it and pleaded with his mentors.

"Drink," his great-uncle pointed to the bottle.

A single tear slipped from his eye, but Pete reluctantly put the bottle to his lips again. This time though he sipped it ever so slowly until his tongue adjusted, and his already burning throat agreed to let it pass.

"Drink," the younger uncle commanded and Pete repeated the process.

It wasn't long before Pete's head began to spin and he could not stand without swaying back and forth.

"Sit," the elders told him, pointing to the ground beneath him. Pete stumbled, forgetting to catch himself with his arms, and slammed his back into the cold soil. As he lay there, he began to see demons. They were distorted and angry, their fangs trying to gnaw at his face.

"White Feather," he summoned his most trusted guide, "help me!"

White Feather did not appear. "White Feather!" Pete yelled more loudly. Still his helper refused to come forth. Pete looked to his left and saw the moccasins of his Warrior Spirit Redbird. "Help me," his hoarse voice pleaded. Redbird did not move.

His uncles took a seat side by side, facing the inebriated teen.

"You cannot summon the Holy when you are unholy," his great-uncle told him.

"You must remain pure if you want to be in the presence of purity," the younger uncle said.

"Drink is a weapon of darkness and like the beckoning of a beautiful woman, many men will succumb to it. With every drink, the temptation becomes stronger until you will no longer be able to deny it – ever," his uncle said.

"There will be many times in your life when it will try and seduce you, but you must remember that to have it, you must give up your helpers. Do you want to do that?" the great-uncle asked.

"No!" Pete shouted, tears streaming down his face.

In the short time that he had tried to call White Feather and he had not answered, and Redbird refused to help him, Pete felt utterly and completely alone. It was a feeling he had never known, not one day since his birth. It left him feeling naked, vulnerable and terrified. It was one of the worst feelings he had ever experienced.

"This must be the Hell that they tell us about in church," Pete thought. He knew right then, that he never wanted to experience it again.

It was true what his uncles had told him. Many times during his life, the dark and evil serpent called alcohol had tried to seduce him. Several times, after seeing some of his friends lose the inhibitions that their own egos used to keep them trapped, he wanted to experience the freedom it brought them. When tempted, he would walk a few feet away from the group and talk to White Feather. Sometimes, he tried to bargain with him.

"I won't get drunk," he said. "I will just take a couple of drinks so I can have some fun too."

In the distance he would see Redbird, his jaw set and his arms crossed, waiting for the decision Pete would make. The silence that ensued from White Feather, and the sharp stare from Redbird, reminded him of the overwhelming isolation he felt that day with his uncles. Remembering that he would lose his most trusted allies, Pete chose to abstain.

"You will always have free will," White Feather told him when Pete would broach the subject, "but as the Great Spirit has shown you over many moons, free will is not always a good thing. Many times it can be a curse."

Pete knew this was true. There had been a few times during his life that he chose to invoke his free will rather than follow his gut, or the guides helping him navigate the world. Each of those occasions had ended badly.

The first time it happened Pete was a small child. One day, as the early morning light began to peek above the horizon, Pete snuck to the river to play. It was customary to rise with the family, read a daily devotional and then have breakfast. Pete didn't have time for such nonsense. It was summer and the spirits of the trees and water beckoned him.

Pete tromped through the waist high grass of the field behind his home and headed toward his playground. Along the way, he found a perfect fallen limb to use as a walking stick. It would also come in handy to stir mud and other debris near the water to help him find stones and crawdads. As he neared the river's edge, he saw what looked to be a black and white cat. This cat was large and had extremely thick fur. Pete crept toward the cat to get a closer look.

"No," Redbird warned. "Turn around and leave."

Pete wasn't about to leave. He could make this cat his pet and his friends would be jealous because he would have something they didn't.

Pete took another step toward the cat. A small twig snapped beneath his feet. The cat, who had been scavenging around the bank, quickly turned and spotted him. It froze and Pete did too.

"Here wesa," Pete said motioning for the animal to come.

"Go," Pete heard Redbird say. "Leave now."

Pete again ignored his Warrior Spirit and crouched down, slowly moving his stick closer to the animal to touch it. The animal stamped its feet but stayed where it was, so Pete took his stick and edged closer.

"Leave," Redbird demanded again, but Pete continued to ignore the warning.

After Pete had moved about three more feet, his stick was within reach of the animal. He pulled it back and used it to upright himself. The "cat" turned as if to run and fearing losing it, Pete lunged to stop the escape. Pete quickly learned that the animal had not been turning to run. Instead, he turned to lift his bushy tail and spray Pete with the most nauseating and putrid aroma he ever smelled.

The spray burned Pete's eyes and cut his windpipe in half, making it impossible to breathe. Coughing and stumbling backwards, Pete screamed while trying to wipe the spray from his eyes and mouth. Almost instantaneously, Pete heaved from the deepest depths of his stomach and threw up.

Pete's father heard the screams all the way from their home, and ran as fast as he could to the river. He did not make it more than a couple of hundred feet however before the stench invaded his nostrils too.

"Skunk," his father said. "Oh no."

His father's pace slightly diminished as he tried to cover his own nose and mouth with his shirt. In the meantime, Pete flung himself face down into the shallows of the river's edge. He slapped water onto his face, trying to get it into his nose to rid himself of the horrid smell. It didn't help.

"Peter!" his father yelled as he came upon the boy. "Why are you here? Why did you frighten the skunk?"

Pete continued wailing and crying, while trying to explain to his father that he only wanted a pet cat.

The father heard the word cat through all Pete's blubbering and instantly knew what had happened to his young son.

"That is not a cat Igvyi," the father said, still holding his shirt to his mouth. "That is a skunk and it sprays an oil to defend itself."

"Get it off!" Pete cried, still splashing his face.

"That is going to take some time," he father answered, sighing deeply.

Pete's father knew it was going to be a very long time and he started making plans for how to deal with the unexpected event. He told his son to follow a distance behind him and he led the boy back to their home. The man ordered his son to remain outside a good one hundred feet from the house. Before Pete could even kick the dirt he stood on, his mother appeared in the doorway shaking her head.

"Oh Igvyi, she fretted, "What have you done?"

"I thought it was a cat, Momma," the little boy began to cry.

In the meantime, Pete's father had gone to the barn to get straw. He returned with a great armload full and laid it on the ground. Pete's mother told the child to strip naked and roll on the straw. Pete obeyed.

She told him to stand up and his father used a long stick to remove the top layer of hay.

"Do it again," she told her son, and made him repeat the process many more times until the straw was used up.

His mother handed his father a large bar of lye soap and pointed to the river. The two trekked back to the water and

Pete's father scrubbed him until he thought his skin would come off.

The stench remained for days so Pete had to sleep outside. His poor father joined his only son to keep him company.

"Why did I roll in straw?" Pete asked his father, the first night of his banishment.

"Straw can help absorb the skunk oil," his father told him. Water will not remove it. Water does not like oil, especially this oil," he laughed.

It was through that experience that Pete had learned skunk oil was almost impossible to remove. Even when removing the bulk of it, one could never completely get it off because it sank deep into the pores of the skin. All in all, it took about ten days for the smell to subside to just a nuisance of an odor.

Pete never again made the mistake of messing with a skunk. In fact, the moment he saw one in the vicinity, he turned and left in the opposite direction.

Redbird told Pete that he would do himself much good to obey the guides' warnings in the future. However, when he was still just a boy, it seemed that his own curiosity and sometimes his ego, would trump their counsel. It was then that Pete would find himself in a mess of trouble.

As he grew older and wiser though, and after his uncles had taught him that his ego was usually his enemy, he learned to question himself to reveal his own motivations.

If he wanted to participate in something because it would make others jealous, or make him look brave or strong, he knew that he was about to enter into dangerous territory. If, on the other hand, he was trying to be helpful, loving, or compassionate, he would take a chance and usurp the warnings of his guides. In doing so, he understood that he might be subjecting himself to danger, but he reasoned that he could not live with himself if he did not help. In the end, he was usually rewarded with a positive outcome or even a blessing.

After all the years he had spent on this side, Pete realized that he could look at most things that others might consider bad, as blessings instead. In fact, he learned a great deal from adversity. He found that, the greater the difficulty, the more closely he clung to the Great Spirit. This led to a stronger relationship with his Maker and a more enlightened way of living. It taught him not to question why.

Even though Pete was the sole remaining member of his family, he had the conviction that everything was unfolding just as it should. Believing the reason he was still around was because there was work for him to do, he humbly accepted the task. Still, it didn't stop him from wishing that his time to leave was near.

Chapter Eight

P ete had finally reached the destination he was so anticipating, the old drugstore. It was the only one in town and had changed ownership at least four times since Pete had moved to Konawa. He couldn't remember the names it used to operate under, but currently it was Stephens' and it had been for about five years. Pete didn't know who owned it. Maybe it was the woman who worked in the glassed in area at the back of the store. She had begun working about the same time the name changed.

Pete opened the old glass door and a gust of wind carried in with it a dry brown leaf and an old gum wrapper. He struggled with the door's heaviness as he made his way onto the red, somewhat dirty rug that lay directly at the entrance. Pete wiped his feet as he looked around. He saw no one except the woman in the glassed area.

Pete liked the smell of the store. It smelled like coffee, chocolate and maybe a bit of Clorox. He also liked the clerks there. Even though the ownership changed, they had been there as long as he could remember. All of them treated him nicely, especially the one named Ethel. She would have his coffee waiting for him by the time he even got to the counter.

"Hi Pete," she would say. "How are you today?"

Pete would nod that he was good.

Sometimes Ethel would share with him some of the happenings in town. He never commented on them and a lot of the time, he really had no idea who she was referring to, but it felt good to be included. It made him think that by letting him know what was going on, she thought he was an important part of the community. In fact, Ethel had been the one who had told him about the rash of robberies.

"Don't let anyone into your place if they ask to use your phone, Pete," she warned him.

He didn't want to explain that there was no way anyone would find his place or, that he didn't have a phone, so he just nodded to her.

"Lester is trying to figure out who it is but he's not having a lot of luck. I'm not surprised though," she laughed. "I don't want to bad mouth him, bless his heart. I know he is doing the best he can, but we both know he's not cut out to be a detective."

Pete did know. After all these years, he had not been able to figure out why Lester kept arresting him. He guessed that maybe Lester needed something to do because there was hardly ever anyone to arrest. Pete agreed that it was not a stretch that Lester couldn't solve the crime spree.

Pete also liked the clerk named Alberta, although not as much as Ethel. Ethel was genuinely a very nice and very kind person. She cared about people. White Feather had told him that Ethel was part Indian, although she didn't really look like it. He also said that she had the understanding of many of the ways.

Alberta was always nice to Pete too, but she didn't seem to be as interested in him or his well-being as Ethel was. Alberta would speak to him and ask him how he was doing, but it didn't feel genuine because she never really waited for his response. Instead, she would begin relaying gossip from around town.

Pete did not want to hear gossip. He knew it was hurtful in so many ways and sent bad energy into the world. So when Alberta was revealing the latest news about someone, Pete only pretended to listen. Instead, he actually silently conversed with White Feather. If he shook his head in agreement with White Feather, Alberta thought Pete was agreeing with her. It worked out well. The only problem came when White Feather was done talking and Alberta wasn't.

A rustling behind the jewelry counter to his right, caused Pete to turn his head and search for the source of the sound. All of the sudden a blond head popped up from behind the counter, startling Pete and causing him to lose his balance. The head was oblivious to the fact that it almost made him fall over. It bopped around from behind the glass shelves on its way to the soda fountain.

The blond head was attached to a teenage girl who was smacking gum while muttering to herself. She had very blue eyes, which Pete found a little enchanting.

The girl whipped around Pete and situated herself behind the soda fountain before he could even take another step. She had worked at the store on Saturdays for at least the past couple of years. He guessed that she must still be in school and that is why she was never there weekday mornings. Pete thought she was nice enough but she never asked him how he was or participated in any conversation with him outside of his order. Pete ambled up to the fountain and its tall counter, which came to his chest.

"Can I help you?" the girl asked, as if she didn't know why he was there. Pete had never ordered anything but the coffee and this day was no different. Still he felt he must answer her.

"Coffee," he said.

The girl turned her back and walked toward the coffee pot on the far end of the fountain. Pete watched her take a cup from a tall stack that sat next to the large coffee machine. As she filled it, he walked to the box of Slim Jims that sat halfway to the end of the counter. He took one and put it into his pocket. Then he walked back to a two tiered metal swivel basket that held many different types of candy bars. He preferred Snickers bars because they had peanuts, which seemed to stay with him longer than other candy. He picked one off the bottom rack and stuck it into the same pocket.

Pete stood at the counter waiting for the coffee. The girl seemed to be taking longer than usual. He was anxious to get the hot liquid into his throbbing and frozen hands. It would make the morning much better. Pete switched his weight from one aching foot to the other while he waited. Finally, after what seemed to be several minutes with no movement from her, she turned and brought his coffee to the counter.

Pete took a quarter out of his money pouch and laid it on the counter. He thought the twenty-five cents was a good deal because the cup was pretty large. It had only been a dime a few years earlier, but Pete knew there was no way a dime could cover the cost of the coffee and, it made him feel a little guilty. A quarter was much better.

"That will be another forty-five cents for the Slim Jim and Snickers," the girl said.

Pete was perplexed. Why was she asking him for more money? He quickly surmised that she didn't understand the agreement.

"I'm sure she will be told," he said to himself, as took his coffee and shuffled out of the store.

Chapter Nine

Pete stood outside and leaned against the brick of the western wear store next door. He put his hands around the coffee cup, slowly absorbing the heat of it. The whole interaction with the blond girl had left him a little unnerved. He hoped he hadn't upset her.

Pete sipped the warm, black java and felt its heat begin melting the ice in his blood.

"Ahhhh," he sighed, while cradling the cup around his brittle fingers.

He continued to stand against the wall while he relished the drink. He thought to himself that since it was Saturday, he should shop for a little extra food to tide him over through Sunday when the stores weren't open. Pete liked that the town's businesses closed on Sunday. It only seemed right since the Bible said it should be a day of rest.

Pete knew that some of his people had a hard time reconciling their original beliefs with the faith introduced to them before the Trail of Tears.

Pete respected Tsisa very much. He wanted to be like Him – kind, forgiving, loving. He also felt a special kinship with

Him because of His abilities as a healer. Pete admired that Tsisa could heal just by saying it was so. He sometimes wished he had that kind of power, but he understood why he didn't. Relying on his guides to help him, allowed his own soul to grow. It taught him to trust. If he could heal the way Tsisa did – without any assistance, what good would that be? Part of the journey on this side was about learning to let go of ego and trust in things unseen – trust in Tsisa Himself.

While some held fast to their tribe's original beliefs, Pete, because of his spirit guides, found it easy to believe in both ways. Although, he felt the new way sometimes fell short in that it did not give any credence to Mother Earth. He loved that the original way taught that she, and everything on her, was a living, sentient, being. Because of his own personal experiences, he knew it to be true. He hoped that someday the world would begin to see it too.

"If humans can learn to respect a blade of grass, they will learn to respect one another," he thought. It saddened him though, because he believed it would be many ages before most souls would understand this. He wondered when, or if, it would ever come to be.

White Feather had once imparted to him that there were many different soul levels. More advanced souls had already learned how to navigate the world and its workings. He explained that the higher a soul progressed, the more compassionate and caring it became. These souls were the caretakers of not only the earth, but also her people. These souls also realized that every decision made in life caused a ripple effect.

"The breeze made by a single feather, can be felt everywhere. The smallest act of negativity or compassion will travel across the universe because everything is energy and energy is everything," he told Pete.

On the other hand, White Feather said that even though younger souls still participated in activities that were all about themselves and ultimately led to negative energy, good energy was stronger. He imparted that even if it seemed as though there was more bad in the world, as long as there were people practicing kindness, compassion, and understanding, good would always outweigh negative.

Pete took White Feather's disclosure very seriously. During his life, he had spent hours contemplating his role in the scheme of existence. His spirit guides revealed to him that he had chosen this life himself. When he questioned them, not understanding why he would want to be an Indian when they faced such hardship and racism, it was disclosed that he had wanted harder challenges to advance himself more quickly. "Hardships allow a soul to learn by teaching patience, acceptance and faith," White Feather said. The ultimate goal of being on this planet is to learn to love unconditionally, like humans are loved by the Great Spirit."

Pete realized what mattered most was knowing that everyone was connected and that no one should do harm to another human or thing. He wanted to be a soul that contributed to the goodness in the world. He wanted to love others as the Great Father did.

"It is hard," he sighed. *"Even after all these years, I still have much to learn."*

Pete wondered if it were possible for souls to perfect themselves in only one lifetime. He didn't believe it was.

"It will take more trips, but I will do it," he pledged.

Chapter Ten

A car horn blared and brought Pete back to the present moment. He finished his coffee and took the cup to a trash receptacle on the sidewalk. Then he ambled past the western wear store toward the steps of the General Store. Pete steadied himself on a brick ledge, which held the large plate glass display windows. He slowly lowered his creaking body to the second and top step. He scooted as close to the wall as he could, so as not to block any patrons that might come at the early hour. He fished through his pocket, moving aside his small leather money pouch, and pulled out the Snickers bar. His feeble fingers toiled with the wrapper until he was able to get a good grip and rip it open. He took a small bite.

He slipped his free hand back into his pocket and slowly fingered the smooth and supple leather of the pouch he had made at least fifty years before. Although he never carried more than a couple of dollars with him, Pete had a rather large sum of money stored at his cabin. He sold Martha and Burt's house after they passed, and he got a small pension from his working days.

His check used to be mailed to Martha's house, but when she passed, the post office kept it for him until he could pick it up. Many times, he would forget to get it. If Max the postman, saw him in town, he would remind Pete it was waiting for him. If he didn't get it that day, he would usually forget it again. It wasn't uncommon for there to be two or three checks there by the time he retrieved them from the Post Office.

After Pete claimed them, he would cross the street to the First National Bank and give them to a nice lady named Dorothy. In return, she gave him cash.

Pete didn't have much need for the cash, so he took it home and put it in an old boot box that Burt had given him. The box stayed under his bed and thus far, the thieving packrat had not bothered it.

"Perhaps it is too heavy," Pete thought, but then decided it must be because there was nothing shiny in it, and the pest found it too dull.

Pete liked to keep some coins in his pouch to buy his coffee and occasionally other things he might find. He found out early in the packrat's crime spree that he had to keep the pouch with him while he slept, or they too would disappear.

Pete munched on his candy bar, chewing slowly because he had more than a few teeth missing. Luckily, most of the molars remained in his head. Others had come out throughout the years and he never saw the need to get dentures as long as he could chew. Besides, there was no dentist in Konawa, and no way to get to the one in Maiden since Martha was gone.

Pete watched the slow moving cars that circled the street. The road eventually turned into a small highway, which led east, out of town. However, most people went to the third and final block of stores and turned around at the First Baptist Church. Then they traveled back down the street to stop at the shops on the opposite side.

Pete looked across the street at the window of the Oklahoma Tire and Supply Company, called the OTASCO store. Pete had gone into the store a couple of times, including once in the past week. The store actually had very few tires in comparison with the other merchandise it carried, like appliances and television sets.

What had currently caught his eye, made him wonder if he should visit OTASCO again on his way home. It was the same big blue bicycle that had provoked him to stop the previous week. The bicycle wasn't like any he had ever seen. This one had larger than normal wheels and handlebars that curled around like the horns of a ram. It also had gears which Phil, the owner of the store, told Pete would allow the rider to go ten different speeds.

The idea of it was amazing to Pete, especially since it had no visible motor. There were wires that led from the handles to the bike's gears. He wondered if the motors were in those.

"Can I ride it into town?" he asked himself. Pete envisioned, not only how much faster he could get to Main Street, but also, how much easier it would be for him. The only problem Pete could foresee was that the bike was really tall. He was sure that his feet could not reach the ground. If he got a regular bike that was shorter, he wouldn't have the strength to peddle it. With this Ten Speed one though, he thought that maybe the little wire motors could do the work for him. Pete decided he would definitely stop and look at it again on his way home.

Pete finished the Snickers and tried to rise from the step. Sitting for that long, made it hard for him to get back up. He was always careful not to give his bones even a few extra minutes of rest, or they would go on strike. However, still tired from his walk, he ceased trying to upright himself and decided to risk a few more moments before continuing on to Ralph's.

THE LIFE OF OLD PETE

The first time Pete went to town after Martha passed, he stopped in Ralph's to see what they carried. Pete had no idea what he should buy for himself because Martha had done all the grocery shopping. She had been a wonderful cook and made sure Pete had plenty to eat. He especially loved her beans and cornbread, her fry bread and her chicken and dumplings. In fact, there wasn't anything that Martha cooked that Pete hadn't loved. She truly had a gift, and he missed her and their dinners together, immensely.

He remembered when only a year earlier, his loneliness had gotten the best of him. He was sitting in front of the old cast iron stove in his cabin, reliving and missing the times he spent with Martha. Each day's vacant time had gotten harder to fill and he was sad, not only that he was alone in the world, but also that he would never again eat Martha's cooking. The realization led to Pete curling up in a ball on his rusty old bed, and crying himself to sleep.

The following morning, after making his normal stop at Harvey's, he ventured on to the drugstore. He couldn't believe the aroma that penetrated his nose the moment he opened the door. Pete inhaled as deeply as he could. What he smelled was the familiar and mouthwatering aroma of Martha's beans and cornbread.

"How can this be?" Pete thought as he looked around the store to see from where the smell was coming.

"Pete," he heard Ethel exclaim from behind the soda fountain. "you are just the man I've been waiting for."

Pete was confused. Surely Ethel had not been waiting for a man like him. He was too old for her.

"Guess what I made?" Ethel broke into his confusion. "Last night I got an idea that just wouldn't let go. I thought that I should soak some beans and put them in the crockpot because something just told me you would really like them." Ethel beamed.

Pete stared at her in disbelief.

"So, lookie here," she said pointing to a crockpot. "I brought them in this morning and I've already put some in a plastic tub for you to take home with you. I'm going to do this every week and sell the rest to the customers." She nodded, proud of her idea.

Pete was in awe. The beans smelled as good as Martha's and he couldn't help but smile when he saw Ethel wrap a huge hunk of cornbread in tinfoil and put the beans and the bread into a sack for him.

That night, while sitting in his rickety old chair, and eating his magnificent supper, Pete realized that Martha must have had a hand in the whole thing. It was as if she had come back just to cook for her younger brother and he couldn't have been happier. He silently thanked her for influencing Ethel. *"You are the best sister ever,"* he told her.

Each week after the first, Ethel sent Pete home with a plastic container of either the sublime beans or a hearty beef stew. She always included a big slab of cornbread to go with it. Pete wanted to find a way to let Ethel know how much he appreciated her and the food. He wasn't sure what to do, but finally settled on paying her.

The next Friday, as soon as Ethel handed him the bag, he opened his hand and pushed a five dollar bill at her.

"Oh no you don't," she scolded him. "Your money is no good here Pete."

Pete would not let her refuse. It was one thing for Ethel not to charge him for the Snickers and Slim Jims; it was totally another matter not to let him pay for the prized meals. He needed to make Ethel understand how special and important she was to him. He stuck out his hand again, shoving the money toward her.

"Pete, don't make me repeat myself. This whole pot didn't even cost five dollars, so I'm not about to let you buy the whole pot. I've got others to feed."

Pete looked at her long and hard. He could tell that she was never going to take his money. A small tear slipped from his eye and down his check.

"Thank you," he whispered.

Seeing his heartfelt emotion made Ethel a little teary too, but only for a moment. Pete had never said more than the word "coffee" to her for all the years he had been coming to the store. The genuine "thank you," he expressed made Ethel feel as if she had just won the lottery. A smiled loosened itself from her lips and expanded until it swam across the entire width of her face.

"No, thank you, Pete." She nodded, before taking her arms and wrapping them around him. She then led him to the door and waved at him as he left the store.

Pete walked a few steps up the street but then turned back to look at Ethel, a big smile still plastered across her face.

"It is true then. I am helping them," he thought as his own smile emerged.

Pete learned the lesson of helping others by letting them help him, on his very first trip to Ralph's.

Ralph's was a place Pete always felt welcome. Most days, within just a few moments of entering the store, Ralph found

Pete to shoot the breeze. Ralph seemed to understand – almost like an instinct – that Pete didn't like to talk, so he carried the conversation for both of them.

That first visit, as Pete was looking over some Red Delicious Apples, Ralph came and stood beside him. He watched quietly for a moment as Old Pete fingered one of the plump pieces of fruit.

"You take that," Ralph said. "No need to pay for it. I want you to have it."

Pete shook his head no and pulled the money pouch from his pocket.

"No, no, you save that for other more important things," Ralph said. "Never know when you are going to need it for a rainy day. Hey," Ralph pointed to the deli toward the back of the small store. "Why don't you go have Morty make you a sandwich too?"

Again, Pete shook his head no, and tried to hand Ralph some money. Ralph still refused it. It was at that moment that White Feather told Pete to stop trying to pay, and instead take the apple and the sandwich and say thank you.

Pete did as he was told.

"Thank you," he said, looking up sheepishly at the store's owner.

"Oh no problem Buddy," Ralph smiled. "It's the least I can do. You just make yourself at home here when you come. I don't want you paying for anything. It's all my pleasure," Ralph beamed.

No one had called Pete "Buddy" since Burt had left. It startled him how much of a connection it gave him with Ralph. It was almost as if Burt had come back to check in and it made him feel better about accepting the food.

Chapter Eleven

That same day, on his very next stop at Mrs. Doodle's Five and Dime, the exact thing happened again. Pete went into the store to see what it sold.

"Hello," came a cheery voice from the back of the store.

Pete looked back into a dark corner in time to see a tiny gray-haired woman coming to greet him.

"How are you today?" she asked Pete.

Pete nodded to her.

"Splendid!" she chirped. "You just look around and let me know if you need anything okay hon?"

Pete nodded again and began to shuffle down one of the store's two aisles. Because the place didn't have tall shelving, he could see from wall to wall. The walls were almost like bookshelves, and were filled with various items, including dishes and vases. The center of the store had a long and wide-open tabletop like display abundant with individual compartments.

Pete saw little toys, like rubber balls and jacks in one compartment, and yo-yos in another. There were kazoos, harmonicas, plastic army men, paddles with a string and ball attached, and many more compartments filled with everything under the sun. There was Elmer's Glue, tacks, boxes of staples, rolls of tape, pencils, pens, and even potholders.

Pete looked over the large display of colorful wares. He picked up one of the potholders. It was bright red and had small yellow flowers dotting its face.

"Those sure are cute, aren't they?" Mrs. Doodle asked from a few feet away.

Pete nodded his agreement.

"Well why don't you just take one?" Mrs. Doodle took the holder from his hand and headed toward the cash register.

Pete wanted to protest that he didn't need a potholder and really didn't want to spend the money on it, but Mrs. Doodle wasn't ringing it up. Instead, she reached for a sack underneath the register and deposited the item. She then turned to Pete, and with a big smile on her face, handed it to him.

"Everyone needs a good potholder," she said. "This will look lovely in your kitchen."

Pete wanted to tell her he didn't have a kitchen, but he wasn't sure how without starting a long conversation. He took the previously rejected money pouch from his pocket and tried to give a dollar to Mrs. Doodle.

"Oh that won't do," she said, shoeing his hand away. "You don't need to pay me for that. I have dozens," she motioned to the pile near them.

"Besides, they have been here quite some time, and I need the space to get some new things in here. I just love getting new things. It feels like Christmas!" She smiled so big that Pete could see the top of her denture bridge.

White Feather intervened and told Pete to take the sack and say thank you.

"Thank you," Pete said, exactly as he had to Ralph.

"You let me know if you need anything else, now hon."

Pete warily nodded his head again and wrung his hands. He knew of nothing else to do but to shuffle back toward the door with his package and leave.

"You stop in anytime you need something," Mrs. Doodle called behind him. "I'm sure that I'll have whatever it is you're searching for. You have a nice day now, okay?"

Pete nodded as he opened the door. When it closed behind him, he let out a troublesome sigh.

"Why are they being so charitable? Do they feel sorry for me? I don't want them to," Pete silently told White Feather.

"Do not feel badly about their gifts. You are being just as charitable by receiving as they are by giving."

Pete shook his head no. *"I don't see how that can be."*

White Feather answered. *"Generosity is the birthplace of love. When others are allowed to give, it opens their spirit in direct communication with the Great Spirit. It is spreading the spark of the Divine. Giving is like a mirror."*

Pete went next door to the First National Bank and leaned his tired body against its façade.

White Feather continued.

"People can actually see goodness in the rest of the world through their own generosity. In order for people to be able to help others, there must be others who need help."

It was then that Pete understood what his teacher was imparting.

"So a*lthough I don't need it, they think I do, and that gives them an opportunity to open their hearts."*

White Feather smiled. *"Yes. Most people are so caught up in their own difficulties, they forget to love. If people will just take the time to look, God gives His children opportunities every day to love. You are to be one of His opportunities."*

Pete bowed his head. What White Feather revealed made perfect sense.

"Helping leads to love."

THE LIFE OF OLD PETE

Pete was in awe of the simple yet amazing concept, and despite the fact it continued to make him uncomfortable, he allowed anyone who offered, their chance to help.

As it turned out, there were to be many more.

Chapter Twelve

When Pete left Doodle's the day she gave him the hot pad, he also decided to explore Pendleton's Grocery. It was the only other grocery store in town and it sat directly across the street from Ralph's.

Pete went to the curb in front of the bank and held onto the lamppost in order to help himself down the step to the street. He watched a few cars pass before he tried crossing.

Although the traffic had been clear when Pete began his trek, his sloth-like speed worked against him. Several cars, going both directions, had to stop to let him pass. Pete worried that the drivers would get impatient, but they didn't. In fact, the first two cars on either side of him had rolled down their windows and were chatting back and forth to each other.

"How's your boy doing in football?" Pete heard a man in an El Camino ask the other in a pickup truck.

"Two sacks but he got hurt in the third. Doc says he'll be fine by next week," the cowboy answered.

Pete and Burt used to attend the games. There was nothing bigger than football in the small town and Pete often found himself counting the days until Friday. Pete hadn't gone to a game since Burt had passed. It was something he missed almost as much as Martha's cooking.

The men continued their conversation, but Pete quit listening in order to try to move his uncooperative feet more quickly. When finally he reached the other side, the cars, which were at least three deep each way, slowly continued on their way.

Pete passed in front of the Oklahoma State Bank. He had only been in it once with Martha. It was a very beautiful place with marble columns and lots of dark wood. It had large vaulted windows and gold and black banisters. Pete felt like he didn't belong there from the moment he arrived.

Next to the bank was the town's newspaper office. The paper published just once a week. It was owned by a local family and was originally called *The Chieftain*. The name changed to *The Konawa Leader* just a few years before Pete moved to town.

Because Martha was no longer able to inform him of things going on in town, Pete, from time to time, would buy a copy. He enjoyed reading about the football games and he also liked to scan the advertisements to see what latest gadgets the stores were offering. Pete was amazed at modern conveniences, like the disposable lighter. When he first saw an ad for one at Hibbs' Appliances, he bought one to light his stove. It was indeed a great thing.

Next to the newspaper was Pendleton's. It was a little larger than Ralph's, but the town's residents were equally dispersed between the two stores. Pete knew he really didn't need to go to both stores that first day. He already had enough to eat with his sandwich and his apple. Nevertheless, he wanted to see if there was anything else there that he should know about.

Pete entered the store, struggling with one of its two glass doors. A lady at the cash register quickly came to his aid.

"Let me help you there," she said, pulling open the door for him.

The woman was small like Pete but several inches taller. She had jet black dyed hair, piled on top of her head in a beehive. She wore a flowery polyester blouse, maroon pants and large black rimmed glasses.

"Would you like a cart?" she asked, ducking her head to get eye level with Pete.

Pete shook his head no.

"I don't think I've seen you in here before," she said sweetly. "Would you like me to show you where everything is?"

Pete was a little embarrassed. He didn't like this kind of attention but before he could answer, she had him by the arm.

"Come with me," she said, while gently steering him toward the back of the store. As they were walking, Pete could see they were heading for a deli much like the one in Ralph's. Suddenly, he smelled something that made his mouth water and he looked around to find the source.

Noticing him sniffing, the woman smiled.

"Oh you're smelling Bubba's famous barbeque sandwiches. They are really something. People stop here just to get them and nothing else," she told Pete. "Bubba is my husband. He's the butcher here. Come on; I'll introduce you. By the way, I'm Millie."

Millie led Pete back to the butcher case and placed him front and center.

"Bubba, we have a new customer for your barbeque sandwich," she said, pointing to Pete.

"Hi!" Bubba excitedly wiped his hands on the red apron he wore. He wrinkled his brow as he came face to face with Pete.

"Say, you're Martha's brother aren't you?" he asked.

Pete nodded his head.

"Bless you," Bubba said. "I'm so sorry about Martha. She was such a sweet, sweet woman. None finer. We loved her, didn't we Millie?"

Millie shook her head as she patted Pete's hand.

"She was a real angel – a good and God fearing woman. I know she was real lonely after Burt passed." Millie added.

Pete was astonished. How did these two know Martha so well? She had never told him about them, although she did tell Pete on many different occasions that he should go into town with her and meet some folks.

"You have to stop staying to yourself all the time Pete," she scolded him. "You can't just live in your own head forever. You need to get out, talk with people, and make some friends. We've got some real friendly folks in this town."

Pete figured she was right, but it just wasn't his nature. He got everything he needed from his spirit helpers, Burt and her. With meeting Bubba and Millie though, Pete was beginning to understand Martha's point.

"You're Pete right?" Bubba asked.

Pete shook his head yes and was grateful that Bubba hadn't called him Old Pete.

"Martha talked about you all the time. She said you were a very smart man. She said you had even gone to college. I didn't get to do that," Bubba sighed. "I would have liked to, but it just wasn't in the cards for me."

Pete nodded again.

"Hey, let me wrap you up a couple of these sandwiches." Bubba turned and headed toward a small worktable to the side of the counter. Pete watched as he took the lid off a large roaster oven and stirred its contents. He grabbed a couple of white bread buns and opened them, sloshing large amounts of red and deliciously smelling stringy meat on top. He closed the other buns on top of the meated ones and wrapped them in butcher paper. Then he stuck them in small paper sack and handed them to Pete.

Pete pulled out the dollar he had tried to use to pay Mrs. Doodle's for her potholder and handed it to Bubba.

"No sir. That is not going to happen," Bubba said, shaking his head. "You are Martha's brother and not only that, I know what a fine man you are yourself, because she told me all about you. She was so proud of you. She said you helped heal folks and that you were always taking care of her and Burt. I'm just sorry we never met you before." Bubba smiled. "We have been missing out I know, haven't we Millie?"

Millie agreed.

"Oh my yes," she patted Pete's free hand again. "I've wanted to meet you for so long, but Martha said you were shy. I'm just glad we are getting to meet you now."

"Listen Pete," Bubba interrupted, wiping his hands again. "If you need anything – I mean anything, you come right to me, okay? I just feel like the Lord put me here to help others," he continued. "I can't heal or anything like that, but I just want to do anything that the Good Lord asks of me so please don't you think twice about asking okay?"

Pete nodded.

After that first meeting, Pete had heard many times how Bubba helped the less fortunate in town. He and Millie had taken in kids who had been abandoned. They fostered some and adopted others. They even took in a mentally handicapped grown man and took care of him. Together they took meals to shut-ins, did chores for some of the town's residents who couldn't, and Bubba even delivered groceries to the elderly every night after work.

Pete's bones had grown colder while he had sat on the steps of the General Store and reminisced. Remembering Bubba and all the other people in town who wanted to help him, a small tear came to his eye. Martha was right; there were some good folks in this place. It made Pete feel as though he had been put in Konawa for a reason much bigger than he could ever know. Before he could ponder it further, he felt a sharp pain run through his left leg.

Realizing he needed to get up before he couldn't, Pete held onto the brick ledge of the store and he heaved as hard as he could until he was upright again. He stuffed the candy wrapper into his pocket, looked over at Pendleton's once more and then shuffled on to Ralph's.

Chapter Thirteen

Ralph's was usually busy on Saturday mornings, even when it was early. It wasn't uncommon to see ladies whose heads were adorned in rollers and covered by scarfs, doing their grocery shopping. Farmers surrounded the deli, ordering ham sandwiches to take to the fields with them. Pete liked stopping at Ralph's probably more than any other stop he made.

He opened the glass door and found a group of women huddled at the far end of the cash registers. They were whispering and poking each other. He heard one say, "I wish she would hurry up, I haven't got all day!"

Pete thought they might be talking about the cashiers, Betsy and Rosanne, who was Ralph's wife, but that didn't make sense. None of the ladies were in the checkout line and the cashiers were on the opposite end of the area, watching the comings and goings outside.

"Hi Pete, how's it going?" Rosanne smiled when he came through the door.

"Hey Pete," Betsy waved.

Pete nodded and headed toward the produce section. The huddled ladies ignored him.

"Tracey's Orchard brought us a late crop of peaches. They are really good," Betsy called after him.

He walked a few more steps before he overheard something that made him stop in his tracks.

"I still can't believe I called Lester on him that day," Betsy said to Rosanne. "I just didn't know that Ralph had told him to take what he wanted. I'll never forgive myself Rosanne."

"We'll it's been how many years ago now Betsy? You are just going to have to get over it. Pete obviously has," Rosanne answered.

The realization of what he just heard hit Pete like a ton of bricks. It finally all made sense why Lester had asked him what he thought he was doing with that apple and then had taken him out of Ralph's that day long ago. Lester thought Pete was stealing!

"Oh no!" Pete felt his heart pounding. *"I would never do that."*

Pete was almost sick with the idea that anyone would think he was capable of such a thing. He knew there were so many reasons not to steal, the least being the karma. Mostly though, he didn't ever want to contribute to the bad energy in the world. In his mind, it was a mortal sin as bad as any other.

Pete often wondered if God ranked the sins in the Ten Commandments. With the help of his spirit guides, Pete had been able to see the outcomes of the ripple effects caused by breaking the rules. From what he saw, each was as equally devastating as the next. He would never want any of them on his conscience.

He was shown adultery led not only to the death of a family, but the end of the self-identity of the children involved. It changed who they believed they were.

He learned that coveting could actually lead to a series of other transgressions, including murder. In one case, he saw a life, that was to have cured a devastating disease, extinguished. He saw that killing – not only man, but even the smallest insect – could change the course of millions of years of evolution. It could even result in catastrophic environmental events.

The bottom line was that God was supposed to decide when life ended. Everything was planned as a perfect balance for the universe, but for some unknown reason, man kept trying to mess it up.

Pete just could not wrap his mind around how little weight people gave to the ten simple rules. Each and every commandment served a great purpose and every purpose was designed to help those on Earth have a better, happier and more peaceful life. He wondered why people failed to understand.

Pete continued on to the produce section and eyed the peaches that Betsy had mentioned. He picked one up and smelled it. He didn't know what the Tracey family did to make their peaches so good, but Pete had never had any better. They were so thick and sweet, that biting into one was like a short visit to heaven. The juice would pour from them, down his chin, as if he had slugged back a large drink and spilled it on his shirt. If he wasn't careful, that's just what it would look like after he ate one. It was nothing for Pete's shirt to be drenched by the time he finished one of the massive pieces of fruit.

Pete smelled the fruit again. He couldn't help himself. He took two, reasoning that he would have the second one the following day while he spent time with the Great Spirit on His day.

"Hey you," Ralph said, coming up behind Pete. "Gettin' some peaches huh? I don't blame you there. I already had three since we got 'em in yesterday," he laughed. "My Lord they are good aren't they?"

Pete nodded his agreement.

"You been doing okay? You make sure you are not opening your door to any strangers. There's a middle aged and a younger woman going around robbin' old folks – not that you're old," Ralph laughed.

Pete smiled shyly.

"Say, you're not leaving money laying around the store for me are you?" Ralph asked, as if it were an afterthought.

Pete shook his head no.

"Strange," Ralph furrowed his brow. "We've been finding money laying in the strangest places lately. Not much, mind you. Sometimes it's just some change; sometimes it's crumpled dollar bills, but never more than a couple." Ralph looked at Pete again. "Ya sure it's not you?"

Pete shook his head again before Ralph quickly turned away to focus on a little disturbance taking place up front. Pete followed Ralph's gaze to the front of the store. After watching and listening for a moment, Ralph obviously surmised that it wasn't anything important and turned back to Pete, continuing their conversation.

"Well, I'm glad it isn't you because I don't want you payin'…"

"Can I have your attention?!" Pete heard a woman's voice come over the loud speaker.

"Oh no," Ralph said shaking his head. "It's Alberta again. Pete, I have to take care of this. We'll talk later." He patted Pete's shoulder before high-tailing it to the front.

"I want you all to know that Ethel has a boyfriend and they are not – I repeat – NOT acting appropriately!" Alberta announced. "She and Festus Marney have been carrying on like a couple of...."

"Alright Alberta, that's enough!" Pete heard Ralph's voice over the speaker followed by a lot of thumping, banging and a microphone squeal.

"Hang on Ralph," Alberta yelled. "These people have a right to know. I'll be finished in a minute."

"You'll be finished now Alberta," Ralph said. "This is a grocery store, not the beauty parlor. Now give me that!"

Pete heard more banging, clanking and squealing until suddenly, everything was quiet again. Pete looked toward the front and saw Ralph trying to disperse the group of women who had been huddled around the registers. He heard Ralph tell them that the show was over and saw him shoo them away.

"What was that about?" Pete thought. He wondered if Ethel knew that Alberta was talking about her in this manner. *"Surely it isn't true,"* Pete thought.

"It's not," White Feather told him. *"But there is no need for you to concern yourself. Ethel can take care of herself."*

So Pete dismissed the whole thing and continued his shopping. He thought about getting an Olive Loaf or Pimento Cheese Sandwich to take home with his peaches, but then he remembered the barbeque across the street and decided that not many things went better with Tracey's peaches than barbeque. Pete decided he would make a visit to Pendleton's after going to Mrs. Doodle's.

Chapter Fourteen

P ete put the peaches in the deepest pocket of his trench coat. They were so big, they would barely fit. He shuffled up the aisle toward the registers and past a few of the women who were huddled again, still discussing Ethel and Festus.

"Well no wonder she always seems so lively," said a slender brunette with vibrant red lipstick.

"If walls could talk!" a heavyset woman in large pink rollers exclaimed.

"I don't think I would want to hear what they had to say," another laughed. "Lordy, Lordy, I'm sure we would all blush," she flung a hand adorned with an extra-large and obviously fake diamond through the air.

"You just never know about people," the brunette continued.

"I'll say," a forth woman chimed in. "You would think at her age, she would have the decency to keep these matters to herself," she preached.

"I'll tell you what..." the heavyset woman shook her finger up and down, "I bet you that Alberta telling us will sure enough put a stop to her X-rated shenanigans," she assured the others.

"Well let's hope so," the third one proclaimed. "This here town is God fearing and there's just no place for such…such… well you know what I'm trying to say."

The remaining women nodded in agreement.

Pete made his way past them as inconspicuously as he could. *"I don't understand,"* Pete said to White Feather. *"How can they speak this way about Ethel when they haven't even tried to see if it is true? They haven't given her the benefit of the doubt."*

"People talk about others to forget their own troubles," White Feather said. *"They also want to make sure that the focus is never drawn to them, so they keep the conversation about others alive."*

"I don't understand," Pete silently told his guide.

"The brunette there, she has been embezzling from her boss for years. The heavyset woman has an addiction to pain medicines. The woman with the ring buys many things she can't afford and never even uses them. And the last lady prostituted herself when she was a teenager," he told Pete. *"Talking about others gives them a false sense of security. It makes them feel that they are in control of keeping others from*

finding out their own secrets. They believe that if the focus is on others, it won't ever be on them."

"Is it true?" Pete asked. *"Does it work?"*

"No, never." White Feather answered. *"The truth will always become known and they will finally see that all the time they spent running from the truth didn't change anything."*

"Why?" Pete asked.

"There is always purpose to truth," his mentor answered. *"Each and every woman here did what they did because they believed they were not loved."*

White Feather said that the brunette had a father who was neglectful so she used the money she stole to give herself the security that she never had.

"In truth, it wasn't really that the parents were neglectful," White Feather explained. *"Her father was in constant pain from an injury. The pain caused a horrible rage inside him. He never wanted to take the chance that he would inflict that rage upon the girl, so he kept his distance."*

White Feather continued his explanation about the other gossiping women.

"The heavyset woman was left at the altar. She believes it was because she was unlovable when in reality, the man she was going to marry was a homosexual who cared so deeply

about her that he couldn't ruin her life by having her live a lie."

Pete nodded his head as White Feather revealed that the woman with the ring had a stillborn child.

"She tries to insulate herself from pain by having so many belongings. She thinks God was punishing her because He didn't love her. In truth, the child was going to have severe medical hardships. He was protecting her from the additional pain she would suffer when the boy would later die. The pain of having him a few years and then losing him would have been even more devastating."

Pete stood in amazement and awe at the intricate workings of God.

"What about the woman who prostituted herself?" he asked.

"She was adopted as a baby. She had loving adoptive parents but she could never shake the feeling that there was something wrong with her. She felt she must have been worthless for her birth parents to give her up."

White Feather said that in truth, the woman's birth father was killed in the Second World War while her mother was pregnant. The mother, having no other family, knew that if she kept the child, she would be sentencing her to a life of destitution.

"It was the hardest thing she ever did but she sacrificed the only thing she had left of her husband, so that her child would have everything she needed."

Pete felt a tear come to his eye listening to the stories of the poor women's lives.

"Everything that these souls think about not being loved is completely untrue," White Feather continued. *"And the reason the truth will always become known is so that, in their darkest hour, they will have to turn back to the One that loves them most. Only through the Great Spirit will they come to realize how much they are loved and, only then can they be healed."*

Pete could not fathom how perfectly planned everything in the universe was. However, he was distraught that its' inhabitants weren't given the eyes to see it.

"I wish they knew," he told White Feather. *"I wish they didn't have to suffer."*

"The Great Spirit is always with them, asking them to give their sorrows to Him to heal," White Feather consoled. *"Sometimes, they cannot hear, but at their soul level, each one wants their secret to become known so that they can finally be free of the pain. It is not easy however because only the bravest*

of the brave are willing to walk in faith and jump off the cliff of the unknown."

White Feather told Pete that in every case there would come a time when the truth was revealed.

"When a soul can't find the courage to leap in faith, the Great Spirit, in his wisdom, will give them a nudge. It is only after they fall that they will learn they can fly, and their reward will be freedom."

Pete sighed and closed his eyes, taking in all that White Feather had imparted.

"It is all so perfect," he repeated in utter awe.

Chapter Fifteen

P ete stood outside of Ralph's and leaned against the ice cooler. *"Where was I going next?"* he wondered to himself, as he often did. He silently looked up and down the street trying to remember what was next on his list of things to do.

"Oh yes, scissors," he nodded his head. *"I will have to hide these better. Maybe I should just sleep with them like I do my coins,"* he surmised.

Pete lifted himself off the cooler, and steadied himself in preparation for the twenty-foot walk to Doodle's Five and Dime. He was looking forward to seeing Mrs. Doodle, who was always kind to him. When he came in, she actually seemed genuinely happy to see him.

Making more than one trip to Doodle's a month was rare because he didn't have much need for the things she carried, However, the thieving packrat had changed all of that and Pete couldn't believe he was already returning. He tried to remember if he had already replaced the scissors twice or even more. Pete thought about the visits he had made to the store in just the past several days.

"Was it Tuesday or Thursday?" he wondered. *"Was it both?"*

Pete opened the door and the smell of cedar and dust filled his nose. Mrs. Doodle was halfway to the back of the store. She was leaning over a small box on the floor.

He nodded to her but she didn't greet him as she usually did. In fact, she stood up, put her hands on her hips, and eyed him, almost as if she were glaring. Pete turned around to see if someone else might have come in behind him, but no one was there.

"Maybe she is having a hard time seeing who I am," Pete thought to himself.

He shuffled a little closer and nodded again but Mrs. Doodle continued to glare. Pete looked down at himself to make sure he didn't have anything on his clothing, and in fact, to make sure he had everything on correctly. Sometimes he found that he had put his moccasins on the wrong feet or his shirt backwards, especially if it was still dark outside when he dressed. Today, however, everything was in its proper place.

Pete felt a little uncomfortable, but surmised that maybe Mrs. Doodle was just having a hard day, so he went about his hunt for the scissors.

THE LIFE OF OLD PETE

Pete found it odd that the last time came in, the scissors had been moved from their normal spot. Instead of being located in the center table, they were in a compartment on the far end of the west wall. It had taken him awhile, but he managed to find them. He slipped a pair into his pocket, knowing Mrs. Doodle would still not let him pay.

Pete headed to the last location of the scissors, which required him to pass Mrs. Doodle. He could see she had been unwrapping some pretty orange candles that had plastic fall leaves at their base. Pete smiled when he saw them because it reminded him of the Thanksgivings he would share with Martha and Burt. Pete missed those times so much.

The holidays with his sister and her husband had never really been about the food, or even the event they were supposed to be celebrating. It was about the journeys through time that they took together.

Granted, Pete had visited Burt and Martha a lot, almost daily in fact. However, there was always something going on around them. Either the Tinsleys, Martha's church friends, or Burt's fishing buddies, were dropping by. If not, Martha was busy with housework, hanging out the laundry, or cooking.

On Thanksgiving and Christmas however, the world left them in total peace. No one was stirring, not even the Tinsleys.

It was during these times that they could sit and reminisce about their lives in Tahlequah and their loving families.

Martha talked about learning to dance by watching their mother at the ceremonial stomp dances. Pete remembered their mother's fry bread and their father's venison with wild onions. Burt told stories of the shenanigans he and his own brothers managed to get into as children.

Both Pete and Burt's eyes glowed when Martha recalled the quiet ravines, where she would sneak away and hide. She blushed and looked adoringly at Burt when she disclosed it was where she got her first kiss, and that kiss came from him.

The three spent hours memorializing the best parts of their lives, especially the past Thanksgivings and Christmases, when their entire extended families were with one another. They each agreed that those times had been magical.

At the end of those evenings, after the turkey had long been put away, the trio popped popcorn in the fireplace and sank into the old overstuffed sofa. There they would sit quietly, lost in their own individual thoughts. It was as if the world melted away and they were the only ones left. Pete could not remember better times.

Mrs. Doodle stepped aside, never taking her eyes off Pete. He shuffled to the compartment where the scissors had been and was surprised to see they were not there. Instead, they had been replaced by pastel bath beads.

"How odd," Pete thought.

In all the years he had been going to Mrs. Doodle's she had never moved anything -- unless she had stopped carrying it and replaced it with something new. Pete also found it odd that everything else was still where it had always been. He guessed she might have moved them back to their original location so he went back to the front of the store.

Pete got to the pencils and staples. He looked to the compartment where the scissors were normally stored. They were not there. He scratched his head.

"Maybe she is out of them."

He turned to go but stopped when something silver caught his eye. There was a lone pair of scissors in a plastic bin, right next to the cash register.

Pete was giddy. He slipped his body through the little opening in the display that allowed Mrs. Doodle access to her register, and reached into the bin. He took the pair and put them into the pocket that didn't have the peaches. Then he shuffled back into the aisle and turned to leave.

Mrs. Doodle yelled.

"You stop right there Old Pete!"

It scared Pete so badly he almost came out of his trench coat. He turned to look at her and saw that she was scurrying toward him, shaking her finger.

Pete took a clumsy step backward while trying to figure out what he had done.

"You can't just do whatever you like whenever you like Pete!" Mrs. Doodle wagged her finger at him.

Pete looked around to make sure she was speaking to him.

"She did say 'Stop right there Old Pete, '" he remembered.

He looked at the usually soft-spoken storeowner and cocked his head, still trying to unravel what was taking place.

"There are limits!" she pursed her lips and continued shaking her finger at him.

Pete was dumbfound and did not know what to do.

"You just stay right here." Mrs. Doodle pointed to the place he was standing. She squeezed past him and went to the counter by her register. She picked up the telephone that sat next to it.

As she dialed the phone, she spoke the numbers aloud.

"Five," the rotary clicked as it reset itself. "Three," she announced next as she waited for the dial to settle, "One," she proclaimed and "hmphed" as she looked at Pete, "Five," she announced and finally, in a moment of triumph, she loudly cried "Three!"

Pete had no idea who she was calling but he wasn't about to move from the spot where she told him to stay.

"This is Mrs. Doodle," she said into the receiver. I need you over here right now!" She sternly hung up the phone.

Pete continued to watch her, still having no idea why she was making him stand there. In return, Mrs. Doodle scowled at him.

Pete lowered his head and sighed. He racked his brain trying to figure out what was happening.

"Don't you do that Pete," Mrs. Doodle warned him. "It's not going to work. You can look as sorrowful as you like, but I'm not backing down. This just cannot go on."

Pete was more confused than ever. He looked down again and started biting his lip.

"I'm telling you Pete, that look of yours is not going to work. You can't make me feel sorry for you." The gray-haired woman stamped her tiny little foot. "Enough is enough, you can't keep…"

Just then, the door to Doodle's flung open and a huffing and puffing Lester emerged, red faced.

"What is it Mrs. Doodle?" he gasped, clearly out of breath. "What's the emergency?"

"Right here," she said pointing to Pete. "I've had it with him. You take him to jail right this minute Lester."

"Okay," Lester answered, somewhat puzzled. "But do you mind telling me why?"

"Scissors!" she yelled and pointed to Pete's pocket.

Lester turned to face Pete.

"Did you take scissors from Mrs. Doodle?" he asked.

Pete nodded that he did and pulled them from his pocket.

"Well okay then," Lester said, "I don't have a choice Old Pete. You are going to have to go with me to visit Lula."

Pete didn't understand why Lester always called the jail Lula, but as long as he had been going, that is how Lester referred to it.

Lester took Pete by the arm and carefully pulled it behind his back.

"Give me your other arm," Lester instructed. "Careful now, don't hurt yourself."

Pete stuck his arm behind his back and felt the cold handcuffs wrap around his wrists. They sent a shiver through him and triggered the icy numbness in his hands again.

"Oh my," Pete thought. *"I will never get them warm again."*

Lester began to help Pete to the door before looking back at Mrs. Doodle.

"Are you sure you want to do this, Helen?" he queried.

"Yes I am," the diminutive woman stated flatly.

As Pete exited through the door, he could see that a small crowd had gathered outside the store. He figured that people had seen Lester running to the store and they all naturally followed. Lester wrestled with the door while trying to work Pete through the crowd.

"Let us through now," he hollered to the lookie-loos. "Come on now, back up. Old Pete is fragile, don't crowd em," Lester admonished.

When he finally managed to maneuver Pete to the curb, Lester looked down at the two-foot drop to the street. He then looked at Pete.

"I'm gonna have to figure out how to get ya down this step without hurtin' ya."

Lester stood silent for a moment longer, looking from the curb to Pete and then back again.

"I can't pick you up cause I'm afraid I'll snap your bones," he thought aloud.

"Mrs. Doodle? Why are you having Pete arrested?" Pete heard someone in the crowd ask.

"Yeah," another person said. "Why?"

"Helen?" Pete heard Ethel's voice. "What's going on?"

Pete looked back and saw Ethel and Alberta face to face with Mrs. Doodle.

"Why are you arresting Old Pete?" Ethel asked again.

Pete heard a most unexpected reply.

"He stole some scissors!" Mrs. Doodle squawked, defending her actions.

At first, Pete thought he hadn't heard right and it took him a moment to wrap his head around what she said.

"She wanted me to pay for them?" Pete alarmingly asked White Feather. *"Why now? I don't understand."*

"Just listen," White Feather told him.

"But Helen, we don't arrest Pete, you know that," Ethel reasoned.

"I know!" Mrs. Doodle exhaled, clearly annoyed. "But he took scissors on Tuesday!" she said.

"What? You're just now having him arrested?" Alberta queried.

"No, no, no," Mrs. Doodle was shaking her head. "He took another pair on Thursday." She nodded as if that explained it all.

"So you're having him arrested now?" Ethel repeated, obviously puzzled.

"No!" Mrs. Doodle exclaimed, clearly exasperated.

"He took two pairs this week already and one last week," Mrs. Doodle started to explain before Ethel interrupted.

"Well maybe he lost them," she reasoned.

"That's exactly what I thought, although I was skeptical," Mrs. Doodle answered. "Anyway, I still let him have them."

"So why are you arresting him now?" someone else in the crowd asked.

"Because he came in again today and stole another pair. Even after I tried to hide them from him!" She threw her hands through the air for added emphasis. "I don't mind helping him out, but that is just thieving to be thieving and I'm not having it! Besides, now I'm out of scissors," she huffed.

A collective gasp escaped from the crowd, followed by a few giggles.

"Pete, lean in to me on my shoulder here," Lester had finally figured out a plan and got Pete's attention back on him.

"I'm going to kind of get you like a sack of potatoes so's I won't hurt ya. Okay?"

Pete nodded and did as he was told. He leaned into the extra-large officer. Lester did exactly what he said, and picked Pete up, heaving him over his shoulder before gently lowering him onto the street.

"Let's go Big Guy," Lester said, directing the ancient man across the street, toward the jail.

Pete felt a tear in his eye. He couldn't remember a time when he was more upset, except of course when he had lost Burt, Martha and his mother.

"They think I stole," he lowered his chin to his chest as shame filled every cell in his body. As he walked, he could feel the eyes of the town on him, and his mortification was so strong that he couldn't even bring himself to protest.

Chapter Sixteen

Lester took Pete inside City Hall and led him into the one room police station. A young, stringy haired girl, sat behind a tall wooden counter at the dispatcher's desk. She loudly smacked her chewing gum.

"I'm going to put Pete back in the second cell," Lester said to her. "Is Bengal Billy awake yet?"

"How would I know?" the teen rolled her eyes.

"Oh you would know," a new voice attached to clicking heels, filled the doorway. Pete looked up to see a thirty-something-year-old woman with hair so blond, it was almost white. She was sporting bright red pumps and white lipstick, which somewhat matched her hair. The drastic lack of color on her face startled Pete, and embarrassed, he looked away.

"Billy yells his head off when he's awake," the woman announced. "You will never mistake the fact that he is awake, ain't that right Lester?" she chuckled.

"Oh that sure enough is the truth," Lester nodded his head, "and you might just as well get ready for it young un', cause it's a comin'," he warned the girl before turning his attention back toward Pete.

"Pete, turn around here and let me get these cuffs off ya," he said, taking Pete by the shoulders and helping him rotate.

After he removed the cuffs, Lester tilted his head and stooped to look Pete in the eye.

"Why'd you go and steal those scissors from Mrs. Doodle?" he asked.

Pete didn't answer.

"I'm sure she would have never called me if you would have just gotten one pair," Lester maintained. "Why did you need all them anyway?"

Pete stood for a moment contemplating explaining the situation, but then decided it would require too many words. He also concluded that Lester wouldn't understand, so he remained silent.

"Not gonna tell me huh? Well okay then, ya know I have to keep you here, at least until Mrs. Doodle calms down."

Pete shook his head that he understood.

"Gonna be lunch time here in a little while." Lester patted his enormous belly. "Guess I'll call up to Pendleton's and get us some sammiches. That okay with ya'll?"

Everyone nodded their approval and Lester passed the buck.

"Call on up there while I get Pete sitchee-ated," he told the girl.

Pete led Lester toward the back of the building. The two jail cells sat across from one another, with only the hallway and the back door separating them. Pete saw the door was open, allowing a slight breeze to cool the area. When he got close enough, he could see that Bengal Billy's dogs were all lying outside, awaiting their master's release.

Lester opened the cell door and helped Pete inside. The dogs, which were piled three high, stood up to see if Billy was coming. Pete noticed that each was wearing a piece of clothing.

"Here ya go," Lester assisted in lowering Pete down on the tiny bunk, which was the only thing in the cell. "You want me to help you get your coat off?" he asked the decrepit old man.

Pete shook his head no.

"Okay, well, let me know if ya need anything and I'll get ya a sammich here pretty soon."

Lester made his way back down the hall, never latching the cell door. Pete found it odd that whenever he was "locked up," Lester never actually locked the cell. He guessed that the policeman operated on the honor system.

Pete looked across the narrow hallway that divided the cells. Bengal Billy was fast asleep. The screen door didn't do much for cooling the building; especially the two little cells, and Pete could see and smell the perspiration dripping down the side of Billy's face. It smelled of cheap gin.

Pete had noticed earlier the nice big window air-conditioning unit in Lester's office. The dispatcher's hair had been blowing the entire time he was in there and everything was as cool as a cucumber. Pete was glad he didn't have to stay in the office any longer, or it wouldn't have been just his hands that were frozen all the way through.

One of Billy's dogs, who was wearing a pair of women's underwear, came to the door and whimpered. Pete smiled at her. She had soft brown eyes, like those of a doe. Pete knew dogs were one of the Great Spirit's most purposeful gifts to man. He also knew that it was no coincidence that the word "Dog" was God spelled backwards. Dogs were a perfect reflection of The Great Spirit's love for humankind and like God, dogs loved unconditionally.

Pete had contemplated this fact many times. He thought of all the dogs he had known throughout his life. He had been master to a few and he treated them with great respect.

Unfortunately, he had witnessed others who had not been as kind and loving as he had been to his beloved companions. Pete had seen horrible abuse inflicted on the creatures. It was amazing to him, but they always remained loyal to their masters. In fact, Pete realized that like the Great Spirit, there was nothing a man could do that would extinguish a dog's love.

Like God, a dog could be abused, neglected, forgotten, denied, abandoned and cursed, but none of it diminished the love or loyalty either had. For a dog, the moment a beating was over, it would slink back to the offender and offer up its love.

It was the same for the Great Spirit. In Pete's own life, he had estranged himself from his Creator. However, when he eventually returned, like the prodigal son, he was welcomed with open arms.

Because of this, Pete revered dogs and tried to emulate their devotion. He knew he never quite measured up to the love and forgiveness a dog offered. He believed that if he could have, he would have been perfect like Tsisa. Still, even though he had often failed to love unconditionally, Pete knew he should try – even when it was difficult. Seeing this dog's devotion reminded him of it.

"Soon," he said to the doe eyed dog. "You will be with him again soon."

The dog nodded her head and turned to lay back down on the pile made by her two companions.

Pete scooted back on the small bunk and pulled his bony legs beneath him. He watched the rise and fall of Billy's chest, while listening to his snores escape in loud crescendos before they fell into flat huffs.

Billy was one who had succumbed to the darkness of the drink and Pete felt sorry for him, but also a little uncomfortable. Looking at Billy was like seeing the road he more than likely would have taken had it not been for the guidance of his uncles and his beloved spirit helpers. Everything they had shown and told Pete about the seduction of the drink was laying there personified in front of him.

"It is such a waste. What would his life look like if he had never turned to alcohol?" he wondered.

Pete had never served in a war but he had heard that many men who did were never the same. He imagined that Billy's drinking did in fact have something to do with whatever may have happened in Vietnam.

Billy had only returned to Konawa, about three years earlier. Before he had left, sometime in the middle 1960's, Billy had made quite a name for himself as a boxer. Pete didn't know much about his sporting stint, but Martha had told him that when Billy left for the army, his boxing career ended.

Pete was sad because if Billy was as well known in the sporting world as people said, then he could have been a great example to other Indian children. It would have proven to them that just because they were Indian, it didn't mean their dreams were limited. It was disheartening to Pete that Billy would not have that effect, and possibly the opposite.

"No judgment," he heard White Feather say, and he was immediately upset with himself for allowing his mind to take that path.

Pete nodded his head and reminded himself that even though something might seem bad, it could be the means to a greater outcome. It was a hard thing for Pete to remember. Things sometimes seemed black and white, but he found they seldom were.

"What if Billy is one who has been sent to give others a chance to help?" The thought made Pete feel better.

Billy noisily rolled over on his bunk mumbling something about someone named Earlene. Pete couldn't understand what he was saying. He guessed that maybe Earlene was Billy's girlfriend, if he had one.

Pete heard someone tromping down the long hallway. Considering how much weight was behind the heavy footsteps, Pete guessed it had to be Lester.

"How ya doin' Old Pete?" Lester half-heartedly waved as he came into view. He stopped directly between the two cells.

"He still ain't up?" Lester nodded toward Billy.

Pete shook his head no.

"Got ya a sammich." Lester held a brown paper bag up and opened the cell door. "Here's ya some water too," he said, giving Pete a half-filled jelly jar.

Pete took the bag and the jelly jar and nodded his head in appreciation to Lester.

"If this un wakes up," Lester said, cocking his head toward Billy's cell, "tell him I got him one too. Say, I know ya probably want to head on home, but I don't think I can let you go today." Lester fidgeted from one foot to the next while wiping his sweaty brow with the back of his hand. "I think if I did, Mrs. Doodle might get purty upset with me, and we can't have that, can we?"

Pete remained silent.

"So's if ya don't care, I'm just gonna leave ya here tonight. I'll get ya some supper from the Eater Upper and first thing in the morning, I'll come back here, get ya, and take ya home. Okay by you?"

Pete nodded.

"Okie dokie then," Lester turned to go, "but no more scissors, ya hear?"

Pete nodded again.

"Good deal,"

Pete pulled the barbeque sandwich from its greasy bag.

"*Perfect with the peaches.*" he smiled to himself.

Chapter Seventeen

P ete awoke with a start. Someone was yelling something about getting out, and in his delirium, he couldn't understand why he would need to get out of his cabin. Was it on fire? It took a moment for Pete to realize he wasn't at home and it wasn't on fire. He was in a jail cell and the source of the cursing and shrieks was Bengal Billy.

"How's bout some damn help here?!" Billy screamed down the hall. "Why the hell you got me in here Lester?!" Billy waited only a second for a reply before ramping up again.

"Lester!" Billy yelled. "Lester! I know you can hear me and I want ta get out!"

Pete sat up on his cot and stared at the still partially inebriated man.

Billy noticed the movement and stopped yelling.

"Hey old timer," Billy said in a much calmer voice. "They got you too? How long I been here?" Billy asked Pete.

Pete shrugged his shoulders. He didn't even know how long he had been asleep after eating his sandwich and the peach. The barbeque sandwiches were known to have that effect on him. They made him so full and satiated that all his body wanted to do was sleep it off.

"What you in for?" Billy asked.

Pete lowered his head in shame. He couldn't even bring himself to say it. He didn't want anyone, even Bengal Billy to think he was a thief.

"No matter, Lester's just like that. He likes to lock you up for just looking at him funny," Billy justified. "I sure need something to drink." He looked around his cell.

Pete bent over to pick up the jelly jar, still half-full of water. He opened his cell door and handed it to Billy through a square opening in the bars of Billy's door.

"Thanks," Billy said taking the water, "but it's not really what I had in mind."

Billy took a drink anyway. He then turned back toward the direction of the police office. "LESTER!" he yelled even louder.

The teen girl stuck her head out the doorway and yelled back at Billy.

"He ain't here so stop your yellin'!"

"Dammit to hell," Billy replied. "Ain't that just my luck?"

Billy's three dogs were at the door wagging their tails and licking the screen. One banged into it with its head trying to get through. Billy turned to acknowledge them.

"Oh look at you purty girls," Billy cooed. "You missin' your daddy? You missin' your daddy?" he said in a high-pitched, childlike voice.

Pete watched the love that passed through them. It was a beautiful thing. There was no judgment from the four-legged companions, just pure unconditional love. Pete silently said thank you to the Great Spirit for giving people dogs to show how much they are loved.

"That black one there," Billy said pointing to a dog in a tank style t-shirt, "that's Earnestine. She's a really smart girl. Aren't you Earnestine? Aren't you smart?"

Earnestine wagged her tail and smiled, a big drop of saliva coming off her drooling tongue.

"That un," he said, pointing to the doe eyed and underwared cross between a golden retriever and a chow, "is Darlene!" Billy slapped his knee. "She can shake your hand. I swear to it." Billy held up three fingers in a Boy Scout's honor pose.

"And that un," he said pointing to what looked like a gray fuzzy cross between a sheep dog and a schnauzer, "she's Earlene."

Pete realized then, that Earlene, who was wearing a pair of denim shorts, must have been the Earlene of Billy's dreams.

"Look at that dog, would you?" he pointed to the canine. "Ain't she just the purtiest thing you ever seen?"

Billy had a smile bigger than the state of Texas on his face. "You're my girls, aren't you? You're my little princesses," he cooed.

All three dogs barked and howled.

"See I told you they was smart," he nodded his head up and down, trying to assure Pete of their intelligence.

The stringy haired teenager came down the hall. She stopped about three feet from the cells, uncomfortable with coming any closer. She held another brown bag and a jelly jar of water in her hand.

"Umm, Lester told me to give this to you when you woke up," she averted her eyes from Billy to the floor.

"What is it?" Billy asked.

"Barbecue sandwich," she continued to stare at the floor.

"Well give it here then." Billy got up and stuck his hand through the hole in the cell door. "Give the water to the old timer. He already give me his."

The girl tentatively moved toward the cell door and shoved the bag at him as quickly as she could. As soon as he took it, she jumped back.

"She's scared a me," Billy laughed to Pete. "You see the way she jumped? Listen, little one, I may be a drunk, but there's no reason to be scared a me. I kicked a man's ass in the ring in my day, but I ain't never hurt a woman – or a girl for that matter."

"I ain't afraid of you," the girl, now embarrassed, protested. "I'm just new and I don't know anything 'bout you."

Billy was already unwrapping his sandwich and took a huge bite, leaving just a little more than half of it remaining.

"Got another one of these?" He mumbled through a full mouth.

She shook her head no. "We're gonna be gettin' you some supper from the Eater Upper here soon though," she shrugged.

"That'd be good. I want a chicken fry."

"Okay, I'll tell Lester." She turned and gave Pete the jar of water, then left.

Billy, stood at his cell door and popped the remaining bite of sandwich into his mouth.

"Man, I love them chicken fry steaks they got at the Eater Upper. Don't you?" he grinned at Pete.

Pete didn't know what a Chicken Fried Steak was because he had never had one that he could remember. Martha used to make fried chicken and sometimes she would fry up some hamburger steak with some onions, but he didn't think he had ever had a fried chicken that was also a steak. He shrugged.

"Good eatin'," Billy said, licking his lips. "Mighty good eatin'. And don't you worry," he looked to his dogs, "I'll share with you purty girls. Won't I? Yes I will!"

Chapter Eighteen

Lester's voice boomed down the hall.

"This day could not get any worse. You should have seen it," he was telling someone. "Thought he was gonna jump off a one story building and commit suicide." He chuckled.

"Oh my gawd," a female voice, who Pete recognized as the blond haired lady, answered. "Why did he want to commit suicide?"

"This is what you ain't going to believe. He actually thought he was pregnant!"

Pete heard an eruption of laughter from what sounded like several people.

"What?!" The blond lady shrieked. "He thought he was pregnant? Are you serious? How can a grown man think he is pregnant?"

"Beats the hell outta me. Apparently, his momma had never had the birds and bees talk with 'em." Lester surmised. "Bless her little heart. She was so embarrassed when he told her why he was going to jump. Anyway, we got 'em down and she took 'em home. Hopefully, she will let that boy know what's what." Lester sighed.

Pete was trying to make sense of the conversation but there was no sense to be made of it. He looked over at Bengal Billy to see if he understood, but Billy was wide-eyed and shaking his head back and forth. He looked at Pete and shrugged.

"I've learned after many a stay in this place," Billy said, "that it's better just to forget it. There's no figuring this town out."

Pete expected he was right. He had seen some pretty strange happenings around too, especially when the Tinsleys were in town.

Pete had to walk past their place each day and it wasn't so bad anymore since they had been made to stay at the home instead of wandering all over town. But before then, he and Burt had gotten into a skirmish with one that the town's people called Trucker.

Burt and Pete had gone to Glenn's Lumber Yard to get wood to build Martha a bookcase. They left the truck parked at the yard gate while they hunted for some nice maple. When they got back to Burt's truck, this little Tinsley was in the back trying to coax another tall, skinny one into joining him. The tall one was shaking his head no.

Burt looked at Pete and Pete looked back at Burt, but neither knew what to do. Finally, Burt went to the side of the truck.

"Can I help you?" he asked the small man.

The little Tinsley growled at him and started hopping up and down on his butt. Then he waved at Burt to hurry up and drive.

Burt looked at Pete again and held up his hands asking what he was supposed to do. The Tinsley growled even louder. He jumped so much it looked like he was having a seizure. When Burt didn't move, the ornery man slammed his fist on the back window.

Burt jumped back, scared of the interloper. Having no idea how to alleviate the situation, they continued their standoff until finally Mr. Glenn caught sight of the situation and went running over to the truck.

"Trucker, you get out of this man's pickup right now!" he yelled at the Tinsley.

The taller of the Tinsleys began slinking away, but the little one – completely unintimidated – crossed his arms, glared, and growled some more.

"If you don't get out of that truck right now," the man squinted his eye and set his jaw, "I will call Mr. Tinsley and demand that he keep you locked up for a week. Is that what you want?"

Pete could see that the threat had some effect. Trucker sighed loudly, pursed his lips and frowned.

"I mean it," Mr. Glenn warned. "You've got three seconds to get out or I'm going in the store and calling. One..." he began to count.

The Tinsley let out an incredibly loud "Arggghhh," before getting to his feet and heading toward the back of the truck bed. He stuck his short, stubby legs over the tailgate and lowered himself down to the gravel parking area. Then he turned back to the three men, lunged and then growled. They jumped back, Mr. Glenn, throwing his arms out to shield Pete and Burt. The Tinsley impishly smiled, revealing several missing teeth, and then he grabbed his friend and took off down the street.

"Sorry 'bout that." Mr. Glenn turned to Pete and Burt. "Happens a lot. He's pretty much harmless – just a nuisance. Trucker thinks that anyone who has a pickup is supposed to give him a ride. If it happens again, just tell him to get out or you're gonna bean him with a bat. He'll leave."

Bill thanked the store's owner and he and Pete got in the truck and left. The whole episode left Pete glad that he didn't drive so that he would not have to deal with the unruly character on his own in the future.

Bengal Billy yelled back down the hall as soon as Lester had stopped telling the suicide story.

"Hey Lester, when you gonna let me out?!"

"Calm down Billy," Lester answered, obviously irritated. "I'm in the middle of something right now. I'll be with you in a minute."

Pete heard another man's voice in conversation with Lester.

"We have a good lead we think. We just need to talk to a possible witness one more time. Hey also, was your wife with you on a death call last night?

"Yep," Lester answered. "Spivey woman died. We met the undertakers over at er house."

"Would you mind asking your wife to come in? We have some information about the Spivey woman we'd like to talk to you guys about," the unknown male asked.

"I can do that, but I don't think she's going to be able to help. She jest went with me – nothin' more."

"We'd sure appreciate it," the man countered. "Hey can we use that empty room down the hall to look over some stuff?"

"Sure thing," Lester answered.

Pete heard Lester ask the dispatcher to call his wife and ask her to come down. "Have her bring Marsha too, and tell her we'll go get a milkshake."

Pete wondered who Marsha was. He also wondered if he might get a milkshake too.

Chapter Nineteen

Bengal Billy fidgeted on his bunk, kicking his feet back and forth on the side of the small bed.

"You got family?" he asked Pete.

"No," Pete quietly answered. "They are gone."

"Well I got 'em, but they don't want nuthin' to do with me." He winced.

Pete saw the sorrow in the man's eyes but didn't know what to say.

"I came back here after the war and we got along pretty well, but that didn't last. They don't like me drinkin'," he sighed.

"I didn't drink before the war," he continued. "Sure, I had a few beers when I was in high school when my buddies would go out drinkin' but nothing like I did in the war." He looked to the floor, lost in thought.

"You see things, you know?" he confessed. "Things you don't want to see. Things you never want to see. Things you need to forget. My grandpa, he always understood, but he's gone now."

Pete nodded his head, as if he too understood, but he knew he didn't and couldn't. The worst he had seen in his life was the passing of his family members, especially Burt, who had cancer.

"That is no way to go," he thought to himself. He still felt sorrow that although, he had been able to give Burt substantial relief with the help of his spirit guides and the medicines he created, it didn't take away all the pain and discomfort.

During that time, Pete spent much time wondering why some people had to suffer so much before they died. He asked White Feather why not everyone was allowed to pass in their sleep as Martha had done; or at the very least, die quickly from a stroke or a heart attack. White Feather told him that every soul plans their exit before they come into their lifetime.

"Some want the time to say goodbye and prepare the ones they love. Others suffer so that their loved ones are ready to see them go. It is their last gift," he said.

It made sense. Still it was hard to watch someone die a slow and painful death.

"Were you ever in a war?" Billy asked, snapping Pete back to the present.

Pete shook his head no.

"Be glad man. It is Hell on Earth. The real Hell ain't even that bad."

Pete suspected Billy was right. He wondered if there would ever come a time on Earth when war no longer existed. He and White Feather had spent countless hours discussing what it would take for there to truly be peace.

"A large part of being on Earth is to learn empathy for others. Until a soul can authentically comprehend the power attached to their actions, the world will stay in a state of warfare," he said.

White Feather explained that at the end of a soul's life, part of the life review served to help teach the exact lesson needed for there to be peace. He said that what most religions taught about having a life review wasn't completely accurate.

"Souls will not only see their own life played out, but they will also experience the effects of their choices from the perspective of those affected."

He disclosed that a newly departed soul would feel as if they were the other person. He said it was the best way for them to fully appreciate the genuine context of their life.

White Feather described the process by saying that if a soul treated others with compassion, dignity and respect, they would experience that person feeling love and self-worth. If on the other hand, the soul had been rude, mean spirited or neglectful; they would suffer the recipient's feelings of worthlessness and dejection.

White Feather imparted that in addition to the feelings, the soul would be shown the ripple effect of his behavior. He communicated that the ripple effect could spread throughout the entire planet and continue for years. He also told Pete that it would ultimately return to the sender.

"Because of the ripple effect," White Feather stated, *"there are not six degrees of separation; there is no separation."*

Pete nodded solemnly.

"We may be just a drop, but we are still part of the ocean. One contaminated drop can lead to destroying it all," Pete thought.

"One act of unconditional love can lead to healing it all too," White Feather reminded him.

In Pete's own life, there had been a point when he had experienced a deep understanding of what White Feather had taught him about unconditional love. It was a transcendental moment that was more real to Pete than anything he had ever experienced. It made his life on Earth feel like it had all been a dream, and that the moment he was experiencing was what was real. His soul recognized the truth in all that White Feather had said, and it was forever cemented inside him.

It happened when he witnessed a birth first hand. Pete had become known in the Native American community for his healing powers. Even though he was not from the Seminole Tribe, most of its members had long ago accepted Pete as their own. They would get word to him through Martha and he would do what he could to help.

One evening, Burt came to Pete's cabin and told him there was a woman giving birth that was having a difficult time. She had been in labor for almost two days. The family asked that Pete come. Burt took Pete to the home and Pete entered the birthing room. The woman was in total agony, screaming from the pain and yet so weary she was almost incoherent.

Pete's spirit helpers told him to raise the woman's legs up because the child's head was stuck above her pelvic bone. He did and within seconds, the child's head began to crown. The midwife took over and the baby was born only a few moments later.

When Pete saw the baby, he was so overcome with love, it was like nothing he had ever experienced. He saw the perfection of the Great Spirit incarnate – a perfect and pure soul. He heard the voice of Tsisa in the child's cry. He was enveloped – no – he was enraptured, with an unconditional love he had never known. While looking at the child, and basking in the love which enveloped him, he realized what the Great Spirit felt for all His children. The all-consuming love left no room for anything else. It was then he realized there was no way that God was a ruler who operated with the fire and brimstone hand he was taught about as a boy. No, his Creator was a being of pure and perfect love.

Pete knew that it didn't mean that, as any good parent, the Great Spirit wouldn't let his children suffer the consequences of their actions. However, the consequences were meant to teach, not to punish. They existed in order to help His children evolve, not to harm them.

It was why Pete now weighed all he said and did. Being in human form, he recognized that he would inevitably cause harm; but he could no longer ignore the deep and convicting knowledge that *everything* he did and said, really did matter.

Pete heard the front door open and the voices of two women.

"I told you not to wear that top," he heard one say. "It makes you look pregnant."

"Well at least I don't look that way all the time like some people I know," came the snide reply of a younger woman.

"Hey girls," he heard Lester say. "How are my two favorite ladies in the world?"

"Lester why are you making us come down here?" The first one retorted, "We was just gettin' to the good part of a movie we was watchin'."

"Well, I told you that the OSBI agents have a question about us pickin' up the Spivey lady last night," Lester answered.

"What question? I don't know nuthin' 'bout her." The woman sounded annoyed.

"I already told 'em I didn't think you even knew the lady, so I thought it would be a waste of time. I don't know what Mrs. Spivey has to do with anything I called them in on anyway," Lester mumbled.

"Why you call 'em in?" the younger woman asked.

"Ta help me with the senior citizen's robberies," he replied. "I ain't been able to get anywhere on 'em and everyone around here is in a tizzy about it. They act like I'm supposed to just wave a magic wand and figure these things out," he huffed.

Pete heard the sound of boots leaving the room down the hall and heading up front. Then he heard introductions.

"Agent Douglas, Agent Brett, this here is my wife, Patsy and my daughter Marsha," he heard Lester say.

"Nice to meet you," one of the men replied.

"I don't know why you want to talk to us," he heard the older woman say. "I don't know the Spivey woman. I just went along to help out Lester. I do that sometimes."

"Hold that thought," Pete heard the second agent say. "We have to do a quick interview. Should take us less than ten minutes. Would you mind waiting for us?"

"Well ummm," the woman started to say before Lester interrupted.

"That'd be okay," Lester answered for her. "Do you need my help?"

"I think we got this. We'll be back shortly," one of the men countered.

"Okay then. At least it gives me a chance to visit with my girls."

Pete noted the happiness in Lester's voice but in his own mind, he felt something was amiss and the air around him seemed to compress. Something was going on, but as to what it was, he had no idea.

Billy yelled down the hall again, dissipating the foreboding feeling.

"LESTER!"

"All right, all right," Lester responded. "I'm comin'. Hold your britches."

Lester waddled down the hall and stopped at Billy's cell.

"What you gonna do if I let ya out?" Lester asked him.

"I'm goin' home," Billy replied, as if Lester was stupid.

"That's what I wanted you to say. No goin' back to the Red Door. You got it?" The burly man eyed Billy.

"I said I'm goin' home. You deaf?" Billy challenged.

"I ain't deaf," Lester retorted, "but I sometimes think you are. Especially when you tell me you're goin' home and I find you back at the Red Door." Lester put his hands on his hips.

"I ain't goin' to the Red Door!" Billy yelled. "Besides, my girls need dinner. They's hungry. Aren't you Princesses? Aren't you hungry?" Billy's entourage wagged their tails.

"Alright then," Lester replied, "but I'm gonna watch you Billy, and if I see you within 20 yards of that place, you're staying here with Lula ALL NIGHT!"

Billy rolled his eyes and Lester produced the key to unlock the cell. Billy stood and stretched, letting out a long and loud yawn. His dogs began to whine, bark and wiggle with excitement.

"Just let me out the back," Billy told Lester, which the portly man did.

"I don't want to see you back here, Billy," Lester yelled after him.

Billy didn't reply.

Chapter Twenty

Lester yelled up the hall. "Look out the front door and make sure Billy ain't headed to the Red Door!" Pete assumed he was talking to the dispatcher.

"How ya doin'?" he turned and asked Pete.

Pete nodded he was fine.

"I've got the girl gettin' you some dinner soon. Anything special you want?" he asked.

Pete was now curious about the Chicken Fried Steak that Billy mentioned. It never hurt to try new things and Billy made it sound pretty good.

"Chicken Fry," Pete answered.

"That actually sounds pretty good," Lester agreed. "Maybe me and my girls will go to the Eater Upper for dinner and get that too. Okay, well, it'll be here shortly." Lester turned around and waddled back down the hall.

Pete heard Lester walk into his office and the hallway remained quiet for several minutes before the door opened again and the two male voices that had left earlier broke the silence.

Pete struggled to hear what they were saying, but he couldn't make it out. It was clear however, that they had lowered their voices in an attempt to keep their conversation from Lester.

"Shhh," he managed to hear one say. "Don't let him hear you."

It was only a few seconds later before they abandoned their whispering.

"Hey Lester, we're back," one of them hollered.

Pete heard the group reassemble and the older woman speak.

"Like I said, I don't know what you want to talk to me about. I didn't know the woman that died last night."

"I understand," the first agent answered. "Actually, we need to speak with both you and your daughter. Can you come with us to this room down the hall?"

The second agent took the lead. "We'll explain everything to you in just a moment. "Lester?" he hollered toward the office, "We're going back to the meeting room if that's okay."

Pete heard Lester waddle back into the hall. "Yeah, but do you mind telling me what's going on?"

"We'll be out shortly," one of the men said, ignoring Lester's request.

"Ya want me to be there too?" Lester attempted again.

"No Lester, this won't take long. No need to take you away from your other important business," an agent answered.

"Okay then, holler if ya need me," he reluctantly relented. "I'll be in my office."

Pete heard the agents and the women walk to the meeting room, which was halfway between the office and the cells. He wondered if they would leave the door open so that he could hear the conversation, although he struggled with whether he should listen.

"I guess if they leave it open, I really have no choice," he thought. *"It's not like I can leave."*

As soon as Pete finished the thought, he heard the door close. He was silently grateful.

Pete sat back on his bunk and again tucked his legs beneath him. He was getting a little hungry and thought about eating his other peach, but he really wanted to save it for the following day.

It wasn't long before muffled, but loud conversation could be heard coming from the meeting room. Pete could only make out a few words, which consisted of "tied up," "money," and "crime."

As he was trying to decipher the code, he heard the older woman yell "Just what are you accusing us of?!" Then he heard Lester head down the hall, stop at the meeting room door, and knock. Lester didn't wait for an answer before opening it.

"Everything okay in here?" Pete heard him ask. "Why is my wife yelling? Why are you yelling, Honey?"

"You are not going to believe this!" Pete heard her hysterically bellow. "They think we…"

Just then, one of the agents interrupted.

"Lester, I'm sorry, but we are going to have to ask you to leave."

"What do you mean? I'm the officer here. This is my station. I'm the chief. I don't have to leave and you both need to tell me what is going on here. This is my jurisdiction," he said more forcefully than Pete had ever heard him speak.

"Besides," Lester continued, "I asked you here to help me with the senior citizen robberies and nothing more. If you aren't going to help me with those, then you two might as well leave," he ordered.

Pete heard the clicking of high heel shoes somewhere past Lester. He thought it must be the blonde woman and her bright red pumps.

"Lester, again, we need to ask you to leave," the other agent replied to his demand. "We are in the middle of a formal investigation and you cannot interrupt that even if you are the chief here. If you don't leave, we will consider it obstructing justice and I know you don't want that."

"You just wait one minute here!" Lester was yelling now. "I ain't obstructing nothin'. I didn't ask you to come in here and interrogate my wife and daughter over a woman who died of natural causes. We told you they didn't even know her. You don't have that right, OSBI or not."

Lester was obviously trying to put his foot down but it didn't work.

"Lester, I'm not asking you – I'm telling you. If you don't close that door right now, I will arrest you. I mean it. This is your last warning," the first agent said.

There was silence for almost half a minute before Pete heard the door shut and Lester step a few feet away. Pete could hear Lester's heavy and labored breathing. Lester always breathed hard because of his size, but it was clear this was more intense.

Pete heard more muffled voices and the occasional shouts of both women.

"You don't know what you are talking about!" he heard the younger one say. Then he heard Lester shuffle his feet.

"You ain't got no proof!" he heard the older woman claim. "Who? Who told you that?" she yelled even louder. "Whoever it is, is a damn liar!"

Pete could hear the agents' deep voices and could tell they were calm, but he still couldn't understand what they were saying.

Finally, everything got really quiet for a long time. Pete held his breath and he could tell Lester did too. Then there was crying – little sobs at first, then wailing.

"I told you we would get caught," he heard the younger one scream. "I told you!"

"I didn't know what else to do!" he heard the older one sob. "She needed them things and Lester wouldn't get 'em for her. She needed to have the same things these prissy rich girls around here get. They ain't any better than my Marsha and I showed 'em that!"

Lester couldn't take it anymore. He opened the door again and yelled.

"What the hell is going on here?! Why are you mistreating my girls? What the hell is wrong with you two?!"

"I'm sorry Lester," Pete heard one of the agents say, "but we are arresting your wife and daughter for the senior citizen robberies."

"What?" Lester said at the exact same time Pete thought it.

"What do you mean you're arresting them? They ain't the senior citizen robbers! That's my wife and daughter! Why the hell would you think they's the ones that did that? That's plum crazy!" Lester was on a tirade. "You city people are plum crazy!" he repeated. "Tell 'em Patsy – tell 'em you ain't the ones."

Lester's wife didn't answer, and as the situation began to sink in, Lester started to beg.

"Patsy," he implored, "tell 'em you and Marsha didn't rob those poor people. Please Honey. Tell 'em they got it all wrong. There's no way my two precious girls would do somethin' like that – no way. Tell 'em Patsy."

Pete heard the woman begin to sob again, and then he heard Lester walk into the room.

"Why?" he asked her. "Why would you do such a thing?" Lester sounded both mortified and heartbroken.

"I don't understand baby. I just don't understand. Don't I take care of you and Marsha?" Lester urged. "I give you my entire check to do with whatever you please. Why did you rob those poor old folks?" he choked.

"Because Lester!" his wife yelled, clearly perturbed that he didn't get it. "Your check can't buy our daughter the things she needs, and I only make enough to buy cheap stuff. Marsha can't wear no discount clothes like some ordinary poor, piece of white trash!"

Pete heard Lester step back and almost fall into one of the metal folding chairs that sat up against the walls.

"She has every right to have the things those prissy little rich girls around here wear. She should be able to have that stuff from J.C. Penny's and The Mod O' Day too!"

Lester was speechless.

"Patsy, Marsha," he heard one of the agents say. "You are under arrest for robbery by force and fear. You have the right to remain silent. Anything you say can and will be used against you in a court of law. You have the right..." the agent was interrupted by the gut wrenching cries of Lester.

"You didn't have to rob them people! I would have taken a second job, Patsy," he blubbered.

"You have the right to an attorney," the agent continued. "If you can't afford an attorney, one will be appointed for you. Do you understand these rights?"

Pete could hear Lester continuing to cry, but more quietly now.

"What is everyone going to say?" he heard the man moan.

"Lester, I'm sorry, but we are going to have to take your wife and daughter with us. Because of the circumstances, we can't leave them here. I know you understand," one of the agents remorsefully stated.

Pete heard the spiked heels of the blond woman walking down the hall, but away from Lester and the agents. Then he heard the front door open and shut.

Mumbling, followed by shuffling and then the younger woman's voice saying "I'm sorry Daddy," was all that Pete heard before the door opened and closed a second time. It was followed by silence, then a mournful and heart wrenching squall, which echoed through the now empty hall.

Chapter Twenty-One

After Lester stopped crying, Pete heard a few sniffles followed by him shuffling back down the hall toward his office. He heard Lester tell the dispatcher to take care of getting Pete's dinner.

"Call me in the morning and remind me to come up here and let 'em out," Lester said.

Pete thought Lester sounded as broken as any man he had ever known.

"Only when a man is down, can he arise," he heard White Feather say. Pete knew that meant that Lester would grow spiritually because of the situation, but still, he didn't envy him.

Pete understood how difficult it was – almost impossible – for souls to realize that the troubles they were facing were usually blessings. If they were ever able to see the situation in a different and transformative light, it wasn't until they were past the trauma. Pete bowed his head and sent a request, for healing and peace for Lester.

It wasn't long before Pete heard the front door open again and the clicking of the high heel shoes.

"Where is Lester?" he heard the white haired woman ask the dispatcher.

"Gone home I think," she answered. "He told me to call him in the morning. I got to go get some supper for the old guy down there. You mind stayin' here til I get back?"

"I can do that as long as you're quick," the woman answered. "The Toilet Bowl is tonight and I want to get there early. This here deal with Lester is all anyone is gonna be talkin' 'bout. Since I was front and center, I know they'll wanna talk my ear off," she proudly declared.

Pete did not understand why people around town were talking about a toilet bowl. *Why would anyone want to watch a toilet bowl? What would it do?*

He decided not to waste any more time trying to figure it out. He looked around the small cell and over to the one void of the former Golden Gloves Boxing Champion. He sighed. It was lonely. He wished instead of sitting in the cell, that he was instead on his way over to Burt and Martha's to have dinner with them just one more time.

It would be getting dark in a little while. Pete mulled over the events of the day for several long minutes and wondered – hoped actually – that this might be the last time he would ever have to spend the night in jail again.

He relived the shame he felt earlier in the day when people thought he had stolen. He wanted to go and talk to Mrs. Doodle and try to explain about the packrat, the many pair of scissors, and the reason for not paying, but he didn't know how. He wouldn't even know where to begin. Had he assumed too much?

His reluctance in the beginning to let the people of the town take ownership of his needs, had slowly faded, and although, at times, it still made him a bit uncomfortable, he too had come to get a warm feeling after they had helped. The smiles on their faces and the jovial tones of their voices had worked to convince him that he was doing what the Great Spirit wanted of him. Now though, he wasn't sure.

Pete's questioning was interrupted by the sound of the front door opening yet again. He heard the young girl call to the blond woman.

"I'll be right back, just let me take this stuff back to the prisoner," she said.

Pete heard her approach by way of a rattling plastic bag and Styrofoam.

"Here you go," she said, opening the cell door and handing Pete the bag, which did in fact include a Styrofoam box. "Got you a strawberry shake too," she added. "Hope you like strawberry."

Pete took the bag and the shake and smiled at the girl. She smiled back.

"Don't go tryin' to eat that whole thing now," she pointed to the Styrofoam container. "It's enough to feed a horse."

Pete nodded his understanding.

The girl turned to leave but then turned back.

"I'll be leavin' here in a little while, but you won't be alone. Phyllis comes on for the overnight shift." She paused as if she had more to say but didn't know how to say it.

"Let me know if you need anything before I go, okay?" she finally uttered, before leaving Pete to discover just what a Chicken Fried Steak was all about.

Pete was upset. He truly was. *"How can I be as old as I am and never have had this?"* he questioned himself in amazement. He had never eaten anything – nothing – not even Martha's cooking that sent quivers through his mouth like the fried steak had.

The Chicken Fried Steak was not like any he had ever seen. It was steak, but it had a batter on it like fried chicken and it was smothered in thick, white gravy with huge flakes of black pepper. Next to it was also the largest pile of lumpy and bumpy mashed potatoes he had ever seen. Next to that was a small mountain of hot, steaming fried okra. The girl was right; the meal could easily feed three or more people. Pete wished, for the first time ever that he had electricity, because that would mean he would have had a refrigerator to keep the leftovers.

"I guess since I'm in here though, I couldn't have kept them anyway," he placated himself.

Pete sawed through the steak with the plastic knife and fork that came in the bag. He sawed like a crazed man, but he couldn't cut the meat fast enough to keep up with the yearning of his taste buds.

"This is something I would agree to live on for," he thought to himself. *"I could eat this for another twenty years."*

Long before his mouth wanted to, Pete's stomach told him he had to stop. He hadn't even taken a drink of the shake, because he didn't want to waste the room in his stomach. Regardless, he would have to. The greasy meat, gravy, and okra were begging for help to get from his throat to his stomach.

Pete sucked at the straw until the thick, liquid ice cream filled his mouth, and pushed the remainder of his delicious dinner to its destination. He was in heaven.

Pete looked at the boxed dinner. It was still so full, it was as if he hadn't touched it. He closed the lid, put it back into the sack, and sat it at the end of the bunk. He had already decided he was going to wait a couple of hours and start again. He was not about to let the meal go to waste. Besides, who knew when, he would get to have it again?

Pete lay down on his side, and pulled his trench coat tighter around him. He took the peach from his pocket and examined it. As he stared at the miniscule fibers of gold, orange and red that encompassed the fruit like a carpet, he thought back to the first time he had ever eaten a peach. It had been almost a hundred years previously when he was just a small boy, back in Tahlequah.

As Pete used a stick to sword fight the tall grasses in the pasture behind their house, his mother yelled for him to come.

"I've got a surprise for you!" Pete could hear the excitement in her voice.

He dropped the stick and ran as quickly as his little legs would carry him because his mother's surprises were always worth abandoning his play.

Pete tore into the small log encased one room house. He raced across its dirt floor and stopped short of the long pecan wood table that his father had made. His mother stood before him holding up a piece of the fruit that looked just like the ones he had gotten at Ralph's earlier in the day.

"Look," she said, bending over to show him the surprise. "It has fur. Would you like to touch it?"

"What is it?" Pete asked, as he put his index finger on the fruit, sliding it down the side, as if petting it.

"It's called a peach and you eat it," she answered. "It's a fruit and you are going to love it."

Pete looked up into his mother's dark and smiling eyes.

"Come here," she said as she sat down at the table and pulled a small plate in front of her. She took her cutting knife and gently sliced into the skin as Pete watched juice cascade through the opening. He sat down next to her as she sliced the peach around its middle and pulled it apart showing Pete the pit.

"This is the seed," she said, showing him the dark brown ball in the middle. "If we plant this, we can grow a tree, and do you know what will be on that tree?" she asked her only son.

Pete shook his head no.

"Peaches!" she giggled. "Would you like to have a tree that will grow these?"

Pete nodded.

"Well, let's make sure you like them first." She handed him a slice of the fruit.

Pete stuck his tongue into the flesh of the fruit. His mother smiled. Then he put the slice in his mouth. At first, the fuzziness of the skin shocked him, and he began to spit it out.

"No, no," his mother grabbed the piece as it slid down his chin. "I know it feels different, but it's okay. Just bite into it as soon as it goes into your mouth." She slipped the peach back in.

Pete's inclination was to spit it out again, but he didn't want to disappoint his mother, so he made himself bite. He was very glad he did. The juice filled his mouth and made each taste bud stand up as if at attention. Part of his mouth was sweet and part was tart. It was like nothing he had ever tasted.

"See?" his mother laughed. "Isn't it wonderful? Aren't you glad you decided to try it after all?"

Pete grabbed for another piece. "Wait Igvyi," she pretended to scold. "Are you sure you want more?"

Pete laughed and vigorously shook his head. His mother returned the laugh and the two sat at the table until they finished every bite of the magical treat.

Pete noticed a teardrop on the bunk beneath the peach. Although she had been gone for nearly a century, he stilled missed her.

Chapter Twenty-Two

Pete heard a car drive up behind the building. The engine went silent and a door opened and then slammed shut. Lester came to the back door, and opened it.

"I know I said I'd be back in the mornin'," he grunted as he heaved himself up the eighteen inches from the ground onto the hall floor, "but, when I got home, Mrs. Doodle was callin' and tellin' me that she wanted me to let ya out now. She told me to tell ya that she was sorry she had me lock ya up," he said, opening the cell door.

"Had ya some dinner there?" Lester asked, pointing to Pete's sack. "Hey, ya got yourself a peach too. You get that at Ralph's? I heard they just got a late crop from Tracey's. I'm gonna get me some of 'em too."

Pete could tell that Lester had been crying. Maybe he hadn't ever stopped. Pete didn't know what to say so he lowered his head.

"Let me help ya up there." Lester bent down to help Pete roll up from his side. "Ya wanna take that with you?" Lester pointed to Pete's leftovers.

Pete nodded and Lester grabbed the sack with one hand while he steadied Pete with the other.

"Here we go again," Lester said as they approached the back doorway. "I don't know how I'm gonna get ya down this here step without hurtin' ya," he said. "It's about to get dark so I don't want ya to walk home. I'll drive ya."

Lester lowered himself out the door with another loud grunt "Ya stay there and let me put this stuff in the car." He tottled to the back door of the police cruiser and put the sack inside. Then he went back to the door of City Hall to retrieve Pete.

"Let's do this just like before. Ya come and lean into me over my shoulder, and I'll set ya down."

Pete shuffled over to the door and did as he was told. Lester gently lifted him and set him on the ground. He then took Pete's arm and helped him over to the car and into the front seat.

Lester shut the door and went to the driver's side. It was all he could do to slide his big belly behind the wheel. In fact, the wheel remained lodged into the burly man's stomach as he sat there. Pete wondered if Lester could actually drive without his hands, using only his belly to steer. The thought made him smile a little.

Lester started the engine and put the car in reverse. He backed up a little way and then shifted again.

"Ya know," he said, scratching his balding head. "In all these years, I don't think I know where ya live. You ain't at Martha's old place are ya?"

Pete shook his head no. "You can let me off there though."

"Ya sure? I don't mind takin' you all the way home."

"It's very close," Pete said.

Pete didn't know how to explain that there was no road to his place or even that he was living in a place he didn't actually own.

"Suit yourself," Lester shrugged.

They drove along in silence for a few moments before Lester spoke. "I guess ya heard all that stuff back there with my wife and daughter," he said, looking straight ahead.

Lester was silent for another moment, lost in his own thoughts. When he spoke again, his voice cracked.

"I never…" he struggled to get the words out. "I just never had any idea. I thought I was doin' good by them two and our boy. I thought I was giving 'em what they needed. How could I a been so blind?"

Pete didn't know if he should answer or if the question was rhetorical. He remained silent.

"I know I don't make a lot of money," Lester continued, "and I always 'preciated that Patsy would work too. She used ta run the swimmin' pool and now she runs the skatin' rink," he explained. "When Marsha and our boy were little, I made sure she got ta stay home with 'em," he kept his eyes on the road instead of looking at Pete. "I moonlighted doin' security at the cup company in Maiden so's we'd have extra money and she wouldn't have ta work," he furrowed his brow.

"I wanted her ta raise our kids. Why else would you have 'em? Ain't right for others to raise your children," Lester veered from the original topic.

He went silent again, lost in his memories. When he continued, he sounded forceful.

"When they got in school, Patsy said she was bored an wanted to work. Said she needed some adult interaction. I told her it was fine. When the kids were out of school in the summers, she made sure she worked doing stuff that they could do too – like the pool and skatin'. I know it didn't pay much, but ta me we had everything we needed. We was doin' just fine. Everything was fine."

Pete nodded his head and Lester looked over at him momentarily. "I just don't know how I missed it. How'd I miss it?"

Silence overtook the cabin once again as Lester navigated the big curve that led out of town. As they passed Tinsley's Nursing Home, Pete looked to see if any of the Tinsleys were out. The town had changed since they were not allowed to roam freely any more. Something seemed like it was missing from the atmosphere. He could see a few of the residents mingling inside the chain-linked fence that surrounded the place. He didn't see Trucker.

"I don't know what I'm gonna do," Lester began to choke up again. "My family is my life. If they go ta j…" the word caught in his throat. "If they go ta jail," he managed to spit out before stifling a sob, "I won't make it." Now the tears were streaming down his swollen face and he shook his head while his whole body followed suit.

Lester turned onto the road between the nursing home and Burt and Martha's old place. He wiped his face on the sleeve of his shirt and gulped some air. His stomach heaved and released it in little spasms. He was like a child who had cried so long and hard, that he wasn't able to catch his breath. Pete had never felt sorrier for a man than he did at that moment.

Lester eased the cruiser over in front of Pete's old home place, but Pete did not try to open the door and get out. Instead, he turned to look at Lester.

"Acceptance can only come from surrender. The hope you seek – the peace you are looking for – only comes from inside, where the Great Spirit resides and angels are at the wait," he softly uttered. "You will be stronger when you are reborn into the new life you must now make. You will find your way," he nodded slowly, "because you are not alone."

Lester looked into the old man's ancient eyes. In them, he saw the wisdom of a time span far greater than Pete's advanced age. He glimpsed the endless trials and tribulations endured by generations of Pete's people, and he saw that they had been monumentally more difficult than his own. He watched, as the same great nation, rose up together in strength and courage, to ultimately prosper. It was then he witnessed a peace – more tranquil than a new fallen snow – assuring him that Pete's words; "Acceptance can only come from surrender," were more true than anything he had ever been told.

Lester touched Pete's arm. "Thank you." Then he lowered his head and sobbed again.

When Lester finally got control of himself, he opened his door and walked around the back of the cruiser. He retrieved Pete's dinner. He closed the back door and stepped up to Pete's. He opened it and offered the old man his hand.

Pete took it and slowly arose from the car. Lester handed him the sack. Pete once again and nodded his thanks, then he turned to go.

Pete hobbled past the side of Martha's house. He passed the dog, which still lay on the back porch. It wagged its tail in acknowledgement of the gentle man. Pete shuffled off into the grass field behind his sister's place.

Lester stood watching him for what seemed like a lifetime. Dusk began to wrap its chilly fingers around the horizon, pulling Earth into the darkness of the night. He watched until he could see Pete no more.

Acknowledgments

First, I want to thank my Native American friends who have given me the honor and privilege of allowing me be a part of their lives. Growing up, they taught me have a great respect for each other, Mother Earth, and all her inhabitants. I feel extremely blessed that we were raised together in our small, close-knit town of Konawa, Oklahoma.

I want to especially thank Roy Boney, Jr., Language Preservationist at the Cherokee Nation, for his assistance with the beautiful Cherokee written word. The Cherokees have their own alphabet so, the words written here are only English Alphabet translations.

Huge thanks also go to Carol Cervi McCurdy for her painstaking work editing the manuscript.

A note about Bo and Kip Whitekiller, two proud Seminole-Cherokee-Creek brothers, to whom this work is dedicated. Bo spent over thirty years of his life in service of his country as an Army paratrooper and combat engineer. Kip has been an Oklahoma City Police Officer for over twenty-eight years. Both are selfless Spirit Warriors whose gift to the rest of us can never be measured. They are also two of my childhood friends, who grew to be so much more. For them I will always be grateful.

About The Author

SD Shelton is the award-winning author of the memoir *Me, the Crazy Woman, and Breast Cancer,* which chronicles two bouts with breast cancer. She is also the author of *The Drugstore Series* and is a multi-award-winning former broadcast and print journalist. She loves everything Southern, including college football, the occasional evening cocktail, and Chicken Fried Steak with gravy.

She resides in Oklahoma with her husband, Doug, and their three dogs, Teddy; and Walter and Harvey (who were born in Konawa and have their own Facebook following under #BiteyBabies).

She loves to travel, explore abandoned houses, and see what's down any overgrown dirt road. Mostly, she loves to write.

The Life of Old Pete is the second book of eight in *The Drugstore Series*. Watch for the third installment, *Talking to Tubby,* coming Spring of 2018.

Connect with SD on Facebook @SDSheltonBooks